J
Sandri

Dedication:
Jenjo
Heidi Ryan
Aarin, Mikey and Doug
of No Other Option
Brandon and Tyler of The Green Room
Ann Lister for being a true friend and for loaning me
her rock Gods. You are my love dumpling!

Acknowledgements:
The City of Flagstaff
Sedona AZ
Universal Studios
Skype: Skype Limited Corporation
Facebook: Facebook, Inc.
Swarovski Crystals: Swarovski®

When Words Fail....Music Speaks.

Table of Contents

Prologue..7

Jayden..7

Chapter 1 10

Jinx 10

Chapter 2 21

Jinx 21

Chapter 3 31

Jinx 31

Chapter 4 38

Jinx 38

Chapter 5 52

Jinx 52

Chapter 6 58

Jayden..58

Chapter 7 68

Jayden..68

Chapter 8 81

Jayden..81

Chapter 9 88

Jinx 88

Chapter 10 97

Jinx 97

Chapter 11 108

Jinx 108

Chapter 12 118

Jinx 118

Chapter 13 126

Jayden...126

Chapter 14 140

Jayden...140

Chapter 15 147

Jinx 147

Chapter 16 154

Jayden...154

Chapter 17 165

Jinx 165

Chapter 18 177

Jayden...177

Chapter 19 190

Jinx 190

Chapter 20 199

Jinx 199

Sneak Peek..214

Chapter 1 214

HARLEY 214

Prologue

Jayden

I couldn't believe it! I had made it to the finals of Singers. I left my small hometown in Alabama to hit the big time, and it looked like I was finally going to get my dream. I was the oddball among my friends, always into heavy metal while they listened to country. I never really felt as if I quite fit in. Add in the fact that I was gay and — well, I really didn't fit in.

I was in Phoenix, Arizona, with the rest of the finalists and I was still trying to wrap my head around everything. The producers had flown us to Phoenix to promote a tie-in with a new reality show premiering here. Our first performance and voter elimination show would happen here. So far, I was loving Arizona.

I peeked in a store window as Evander, another guy in the finals, and I wandered around a mall. We hit the game store and I bought a few I needed to bring my collection up to date. Evander was busy checking out his purchases as I decided which store to head to next. I noticed two guys pass us on their way into the store we'd just left; we nearly collided. I zoned in on one of them and gasped as I recognized him. It was fucking Jinx Jett of Skull Blasters! My heart stopped and then nearly exploded as I swatted Evander's shoulder.

"What, dude?"

"Oh. My. God. That's Jinx Jett!"

"Well damn, Jayden — go say hi before you wet yourself!" Evander was laughing at me.

I walked back toward them and realized Gareth Wolf was the guy with Jinx. He had become a role model for me recently. I had come out because Gareth had the balls to do it. That didn't win me any points with my family, and that gave me the nerve to leave for California, to make it big.

"Oh my God! You're Jinx Jett!" I practically screamed.

"He is." Gareth Wolf nodded with a smile.

"Can I have your autograph?"

"Um, sure. What's your name?" Jinx checked his pockets.

"I have a pen. It's Jayden. J-A-Y-D-E-N. Can you sign my shirt?"

"Sure."

"Can you sign it too, Gareth?"

"You bet."

"This is so awesome! I love you guys!" I exclaimed. "I can't believe you're just walking around the mall!" I didn't even care that I sounded like a 12-year-old girl.

Jinx finished signing his name and handed the pen back. I swear to God, I wanted to jump his bones right there in the mall. "Um, so, thanks a lot, you guys. You're so cool." I began walking backwards.

"How about a picture?" Gareth asked almost as an afterthought, it seemed.

Oh my God. I was going to pass out. "Really?!"

"Sure," Gareth shrugged.

I all but squealed and handed my phone to Evander. I got in the middle of them and smiled. The flash went off and I took the phone from Evander, making sure it came out okay.

"Thank you so much," I must have said for the umpteenth time.

"No problem," Jinx mumbled.

Evander tugged on me to go but I kept sneaking peeks at Jinx Jett over my shoulder. The guy was so damn fine it should be illegal. I had wanted him from the second I had heard his drum solo on the first album. The guy was seriously talented. Then when I Googled him? Holy shit, he was gorgeous!

Evander and I went back to the hotel and cleaned up for the night's show. The ballroom was crowded as the judges took their seats. I fidgeted nervously as the judge from England began reading off who was staying and who was going.

"Jayden Dempsey, Evander Torrin, and the Spiros twins will be staying on, but there's a twist, boys. You four will form a band." The judge smiled.

"Excuse me?" I stammered.

"I see more potential putting you together than I see any of you going solo," he explained. "I suggest you boys get some rest. We'll be knocking out a track by next week."

One month later, we won the contest. I was now one quarter of London Boys, a boy band. I guess I couldn't complain. I wanted the dream and now I had it. I was out of Alabama and making a name for myself. I had groupies and now I was the one signing autographs. It was all surreal. I talked over my sexuality with our manager and he gave me the green light. I came out in public and never looked back. I haven't heard a peep from my parents, even after I had a moving truck go to their house for my belongings.

This was my life now.

I was going to embrace it.

Chapter 1

Jinx

I squirmed on the chair for the thousandth time. How did I get myself into these situations? Okay, I knew how. But still, I used condoms and I've been really careful. I leaned over and peered at the sign-in desk at my doctor's office. I had been sitting there for about ten minutes. Why did they give you an appointment time if they're not going to see you at that time? And why make you get there early? So you could sit around longer and ponder your malady?

Doctors are sadomasochists.

I discreetly scratched at my ball sack through my jeans. I had a feeling I had crabs. I didn't want to look too closely, though, because that shit freaked me the fuck out. It was like walking through a spider web — you never know if that spider is on you somewhere.

I shivered.

I was bad, I would admit it. I liked sex. I was Jinx Jett, for fuck's sake. I was a drummer with a healthy libido. I found it funny that these days I couldn't keep chicks off me, when back in high school, they wouldn't give me the time of day. As a teenager, I had acne so bad I really did resemble a pizza — and don't get me started on how shy I was. My parents didn't have a lot of money, so I was reduced to putting toothpaste on my face at night in hopes that it would clear up my face. Thank God for the guys. I would have never made it through school without Ransom, Harley, Rebel, Gareth, and Paul.

Paul.

Thinking about that still makes me sad. Paul Vincent was one of our best friends growing up. None of us had any idea that he'd had a huge crush on Ransom Fox, and apparently still does. When Ransom's little brother, Gareth Wolf, took over for Paul after a nasty accident crippled his hand, we thought Paul was satisfied with being Skull Blasters' manager. Turns out he wasn't, and had been secretly trying to come back as our lead guitarist. Gareth had filled that role quite capably.

I never would have suspected Paul of being the one who was threatening Gareth after he came out as gay. Apparently, he hoped it would be enough to scare Gareth into leaving Skull Blasters. Wrong. Paul was at a private mental hospital in California while the rest of us worked on recording a new album. Gareth fell in love with his bodyguard, Axel Blaze, and they got married.

The doctor's office's radio station was playing refreshing and relaxing "at work" songs, and I cocked an eyebrow as the DJ began talking about some band that had gone to number one within weeks.

"*And now, the number one hit from London Boys!*"

Digitized music began streaming from the speaker above me and I recoiled in horror as boy band music filled my ears. I had no use for them, because as far as I was concerned, they didn't have any real talent. They just stood around a mic, sang na-na-na-naaa and pocketed the paycheck. I stood up, suddenly desperate to be anywhere but here.

"Can someone please rod my cock so I can get the hell out of here?" A nurse looked up from the desk and winked. "He's ready for you, Jinx."

"Oh, thank God." I practically ran back to the exam room and hopped on the paper-covered table. We'd known Doc Mathis since we were kids. I always expected him to give me a lollipop when he was done.

"So, Josiah." Dr. Mathis held my file folder as he turned to face me. He still called me by my real name, even though he knew I hated it. He was close to sixty now, but still had a wicked sense of humor when it came to me. "What have you gotten your dick into this time?"

"My dick didn't get into anything, but my pubes might have."

"Uh oh." Dr. Mathis clucked his tongue as he observed me. "Did we use condoms?"

"We did," I affirmed. "But this might be something even condoms can't control."

"Well, drop trou and assume the position."

"Gee, Doc. How romantic."

I did as I was told and Doc Mathis inspected my backside first. I know I should have been a little weirded out, but like I said, I'd known the man for years.

"Did you get a prostate exam last time?"

"Um, yeah." I bit my lip. I hated those fucking things. I was only thirty, but prostate cancer ran in my family, so early and often was the best defense. Lucky me.

"No, you didn't," Doc Mathis laughed behind me. "Why do you even try to lie to me, Josiah?"

"Habit?"

"I've got your records and trust me, I may be old, but I'm not senile."

Behind me, I heard the snap of a rubber glove and a snick of lube. I closed my eyes tightly and grabbed hold of the table. A finger breached my hole and I hissed.

"I better get dinner or flowers out of this."

"I've got a special balloon for you," Doc Mathis chuckled behind me.

"More condoms?" I relaxed as his finger receded from my hole.

"Of course." Doc removed his glove and dropped it in the trashcan by the wall. He washed his hands thoroughly, then turned back to me and picked up my folder. "I want to run some blood tests just to rule anything else out. Now, show me your pubes."

I faced the doctor and motioned to my crotch. "It itches."

Doc squatted with his face right in my junk. "Ah, yes. I do see the problem."

"It's … crabs, isn't it?"

"I'm afraid you do, indeed, have pubic lice. I'm going to prescribe Malathion lotion. Read the directions carefully."

"Am I going to have to shave?" I covered my crotch with a look of horror.

"No."

"Good." I yanked my underwear and pants up, fumbling with my zipper as Doc Mathis crossed the room to write out my prescription.

"Josiah, please be careful in your sexual escapades. Just because women throw themselves at you doesn't mean you have to catch every single one of them."

"But it's so much fun." I winked at the old man.

"Go see Nurse Alice for the blood draw." Doc handed me my prescription.

"Does it have to be Alice? She loves poking me relentlessly." I scowled and tucked the prescription into my pocket.

"Give her some time. She gets nervous around you."

Doc Mathis moved and I caught sight of my reflection in the mirror. I *was* ruggedly handsome, dammit. My hair was chestnut brown with almost blond highlights and my eyes were the color of an overcast sky — or so I'd been told. They were grayish-blue. I tilted my head, admiring my reflection. I did that a lot now. I was still not used to seeing grown-up me looking so good. Sometimes I still see pizza-face me in the mirror. I smiled and straight white teeth sparkled back at me. Those had cost me a small fortune.

"Josiah, are you quite done admiring yourself?" Doc Mathis inquired drily.

"I'm still not used to it," I admitted.

"I always knew you'd be a looker, Josiah. You went through what all teenagers go through, that horrible awkward stage where you're a bit fluffy and not so..." Doc Mathis tapped his chin in thought. "Comfortable in your skin."

"Yes, well, that Josiah couldn't get a date to save his life. I didn't even have friends who were girls. None of them wanted to be seen with me."

"Well, you don't have that problem now. Please remember to always protect yourself and the women you are with."

"Thanks, Doc." I jerked my chin to the door. "I'll just go see the blood sucker now."

Doc Mathis frowned and I took that moment to make my escape. I exited the room and ran right into nurse Alice, who promptly took me by my elbow and sat me down in the blood-letting chair. I stuck my right arm out and waited for her to cut off my blood flow. My right hand tingled as she tapped on my veins.

"You know, it's not difficult to find them. They do actually stand up and shout, 'pick me'!" I leveled a glare at her as she swabbed the area.

She shoved the needle in and I hissed between my teeth. I didn't know why this woman loved using me as a pincushion. I got a cotton ball and a cartoon Band-Aid and was on my way. I left the doc's office and enjoyed the pale blue sky and a slight breeze. Damn, I loved Flagstaff.

After stopping by the pharmacy, I headed home. We were still recording tracks for the new album, but I needed to get home and get rid of the infestation setting up shop in my crotchal region. I lived on the opposite side of town from the rest of the guys. My parents still lived near downtown Flag. As much as I loved them, I needed some space. Pine trees surrounded my house, which was on a dead-end street. I had it painted beige with mocha shutters after I bought it. A cobblestone driveway leads right up to my garage, and a wraparound deck completed the setting. It really was beautiful and it fit me perfectly.

I pulled my black Ford Raptor into my heated garage and closed the door behind me. The temperature was beginning to drop and snow would be falling soon. I stepped into my mudroom and kicked off my biker boots. I threw my keys into the bowl by the side door and headed for the kitchen. My phone shrilled in my pocket and I grabbed it, checking the caller I.D. Ransom. I smiled and swiped "talk."

"Yo."

"Dude, are you coming tonight?"

"I can't. I don't want my little crabs scampering off and taking new residence on your ass."

"Fuck me, dude. That's nasty."

"Better than something *really* bad," I chuckled.

"Okay. The guys and I will work on the stuff we put together last week. How long until your, um, visitors are gone?"

"Not sure. I'm going to look at the medicine and get right on that, Cap."

"I hope they're gone by Friday. Stan wants to talk to us about some show that wants to book us."

"Damn! Can't we just relax?"

"We have been, or did you forget? Maybe fucking all those chicks is taking a toll on you, bad boy."

"Yeah, yeah, I'm a slut and blah, blah, blah. See you Friday, bitch."

I hung up and rummaged through my fridge for food. I grabbed a frozen meal and shoved it in the microwave as I poured myself a drink. I wasn't a big drinker; like the rest of the guys, I don't like being off balance. I flopped onto my couch and grabbed the remote, turning it to one of the new music shows that began airing last year. I really liked the judges; they didn't pull any punches and tell it like it is.

There were six acts in the finals, and two of them were heavy metal rocker guys. The first guy had a scratchy voice like Ransom's; he could hit some pretty high notes, too. I reclined and turned up the volume. The second guy was pretty impressive as well. His black hair fell into his equally black eyes. He was tatted to hell and had some interesting piercings. Both of them played the guitar and could also play bass. I was impressed.

My food beeped and I trudged to the kitchen, pulled the tray out, and grabbed a fork on my way back to the living room. My house wasn't huge, but it was just right for me. Three bedrooms: one held my drum set, one was a workout room, and the third was my master bedroom. My living room was sunken with cherry hardwood floors and an area rug right in front of the couch. My two side tables were old wine barrels, as was my coffee table. I had a wood burning stove installed last year and I loved it — makes my place feel like a log cabin somehow. I wasn't ready to swing from branches like Gareth and his treehouse, but a log cabin at some point would be nice. My whole house smelled like seasoned wood and I fucking loved it.

My other house was in Anthem, Arizona. I chose it because it wasn't directly in Phoenix, but it was close enough to the airport. Although, these days we just flew right into Flagstaff if we were all going to our houses here. I really needed to head down to my other house; I'd been gone for over six months and I was sure it was breeding something.

I was just about to take a bite of my meal when my phone beckoned again. I stared at the caller I.D. and contemplated letting it go to voicemail. My mother was calling and our conversations were never short. I swiped "talk" and waited for the tirade.

"Hey, Ma."

"Josiah! We haven't seen you at all since you came off your tour! Are you okay?"

"I'm good, Ma. Just settling in to watch some TV and then heading to bed." That was a lie. I was going to take care of the guests that were using me as a condo.

"Well, can we see you this weekend? There are still some of your old things here in the attic."

"Sure, Ma. I'll call you, okay?"

"You be good!"

"I will. Love you, Ma."

I hung up and then stared at my phone. That had to have been the shortest phone conversation with my mother, ever. It then occurred to me that I was sitting on my furniture and walking around my house with fucking crabs.

Fuck.

I put my food back in the microwave and headed to my room. My king-sized bed was against one wall, flanked with two side tables. A sixty-inch, wall-mounted, flat-screen TV was directly opposite with bookshelves containing my DVD collection on each side.

I stepped into the bathroom and tossed my clothing in the corner. It would have to be washed; I didn't want my visitors crawling all over my house. I stood over the toilet to take a piss and looked down. Baaaad idea. I had great eyesight, so the first thing I saw was a bug crawling along my pubes. I reached for my electric razor and just started shaving it all off. I manscaped, don't get me wrong, but I did like hair in certain places. Some guys shave it *all* off, but I just couldn't. I liked a little hair on my chest and … junk. As soon as I was satisfied I'd gotten most of the fuckers, I flushed and stepped into my shower. I turned on the water as hot as I could take it. I scrubbed down and took special care around my nuts. By the time I got out of the shower, my skin was red and pissed. I grabbed the lotion and slathered it around my pubic area.

"God help me, these fuckers better be gone by the weekend."

I called my housekeeper and told her I'd be gone for the rest of the week and could she please bomb my house with something to get rid of lice. I wasn't going to elaborate on what kind of lice. I also told her to wash everything in boiling hot water. She didn't question me and, thank God for small favors, she agreed. I fell into bed and stared at the ceiling. Maybe I needed to slow down a bit on the fucking? I'd been lucky, as far as not catching anything that couldn't be treated with medication goes. Pissing fire wasn't fun.

I rolled to my side with a sigh. I tried once in middle school to ask a girl out to a school dance and she laughed in my face. It didn't get better; I was gun shy and quiet after that. Girls just weren't in the cards for me. Luckily, I wasn't bullied much. Rebel made sure of that. He was the only one who actually looked the part of a heavy metal band rocker. Back in the day, his quiet demeanor and piercing stare could scare anyone. People thought he was nuts and he used it to his advantage. I chuckled at the thought. Rebel actually brought a bat to school once and bit off its head, Ozzy style. Of course, it was made of candy, but no one knew that.

My phone dinged and I picked it up off the end table. Speak of the devil.

"Rebel."

"Mr. Crabs."

"Oh, ha ha."

"I'd like a crabby patty."

"Word spreads fast."

"So do crabs."

"What do you want, asshole?"

Sniffling came over the line and I rolled my eyes.

"I missed you man. Why are you so mean?"

"Stop fucking around. I'm already in a shitty mood and now I'm going to be itching even more."

"Oh hell. You *shaved*?"

"I didn't have to, but when I saw them crawling around, it freaked me out."

"Dude. I can't even imagine. I'll see you this weekend though, right?"

"Only if I get rid of these fuckers."

"Dude," Rebel laughed.

"Oh fuck off. Night!"

I hung up and turned my phone off. I knew I got myself into this shit, but it would be nice if the guys were a little more sympathetic. I hadn't heard from Harley, so that was a good sign. He couldn't say shit anyway; he has had his share of maladies. I closed my eyes and tried hard not to think about little bugs crawling on my nuts, and then I remembered I had food sitting in the microwave.

"Fuck."

Chapter 2

Jinx

I woke up with a burning crotch. Fuck! I was supposed to wash the shit off after 8 to 12 hours. I sprinted to the bathroom, took down the showerhead, and sprayed my crotch with warm water for at least five minutes. My skin was red and angry looking. Great. That was all I needed, blisters on my fucking dick. I hopped out of the shower and toweled off, walking into my bedroom to get my clothes. My housekeeper walked into my room and her scream almost broke my eardrums.

"Jesus, Mr. Jett! You scared me!"

"Sorry! I'm just going to get dressed, then I'll be out of your hair. There's a pile of clothing in my bathroom; please make sure my sheets and towels are washed in the hottest water."

"You already told me that, but no problem," she smiled.

I grabbed my wallet, phone, and keys and headed out to the garage. I had clothes at my Anthem house, so I didn't need to pack a bag. I hit the highway and scanned my satellite radio stations before I stopped on an interview that was already in progress. I tapped my thumbs on the steering wheel as I navigated the twists and turns of the Seventeen. My head snapped up when one of the guys being interviewed said my name.

"So, Jinx Jett was your role model?" The interviewer encouraged whoever it was to go on.

"Oh, always! I loved his drum solo on their first album! He's just so talented; his hands fly and he gets this incredible look on his face."

"Sounds like you might have a crush," the interviewer chuckled.

"Have you *seen* the guy?"

"Let's take a break guys. We'll be right back, folks!"

I wanted to hear more of the interview. Call me vain, but now I wanted to know who was talking about me. His voice sounded, I don't know, country? Not full-blown country, but a hint of an accent. Southern?

I laughed at myself and pulled off to get gas and a drink. I tugged my Arizona Cardinals cap low on my forehead and sauntered into the gas station. I was lucky enough that most of the time, people had no idea who I was — and that was just fine by me. When Gareth came out, the poor guy was dragged through every damn tabloid in existence. He couldn't go anywhere. Thankfully, he has one hell of an intimidating husband in Axel, who is now the band's chief of security.

Our fulltime bodyguards — Achilles, Hammer, and Buster — stay busy keeping an eye on Ransom, Harley and Rebel. Lucky me gets to fly solo for a bit — although I was sure Axel had a tail on me. He always did. As long as they stayed out of my field of vision, I didn't care who he put on me.

I slid back into the truck and fired her up just in time to hear the interview wrap up. Damn. I really wanted to know who the guy was.

I flew the rest of the way to Anthem. I just wanted to get home and soak my dick and nuts in a warm tub. My Anthem house is just like my Flagstaff house as far as size. I have a pool in the backyard with waterfalls on either side, crawling rose bushes all along the back wall and a sunken fire pit with rock benches.

I smiled as I took the Anthem Way exit. I missed my house out here. I had solar panels installed while we were on tour and I was itching to see how it looked. I shifted in my seat. Unfortunate choice of words.

I turned onto my street and for the thousandth time, chuckled at the name. I always say I live on Cock Street, but it's really Shinnecock. Yes, I did pick that house because of the name of the street. I was fucking warped that way. I pulled into the driveway and waited for the garage door to open completely before entering. I cut the engine and jumped out of the seat, excited to see how the house looked.

I stepped into the side room and looked around. A huge, chocolate-brown L-shaped sectional surrounded my TV, fireplace, and coffee table, and the whole area had an open floor plan. I tossed my keys onto the couch and crossed into the kitchen. Stainless steel fridge, stove, and dishwasher occupied one wall, and on the opposite side was a row of cabinets. The island had a no-touch faucet and double deep sinks. I grabbed water out of the fridge and headed to the back yard.

I opened the sliding glass door and immediately felt relaxed. The pool was so perfect it looked as if it belonged in a beer commercial, and everything looked freshly watered. I shielded my eyes from the sun so I could see the new solar panels lining one side of the roof. I felt ecologically proud of myself. I also felt hungry as my growling stomach reminded me I'd only had coffee this morning. I stepped back in the house and searched my fridge for food. I had some old cheese and mustard. I scowled and looked at the time; I could hit the pizza joint and then crash.

I ended up on my bed, munching on pizza and flipping through TV channels. I landed on one with two guys kissing and I leaned forward, tilting my head as I watched them. Ever since I'd found out Gareth was gay, I had gotten more curious about it.

I thought back to the first time I'd *really* been attracted to a guy. It had to be the guy Gareth and I had run into at the mall, the guy who wanted my autograph. I'd found men attractive before, don't get me wrong, but the guy at the mall was the first guy I'd really looked at in *that* way. The way where I was thinking what it would be like to sink my cock in his ass. Fuck that thing was perky as hell; I'd never seen an ass that … bubbly. Plus, the guy was seriously sexy, blond hair tapered on the sides, gelled on the top, with blue eyes so clear you'd think they were ice. I fidgeted on the bed as my dick decided to spring to life. I gripped it through my jeans and squeezed, my eyes closing as sweet heat pooled in my balls. I needed release, but I was afraid to look too closely at my dick and balls. The fuckers should be gone, right?

I spent the rest of the afternoon cleaning and tuning my drum set. I had three of them, actually — the one that goes on tour with me, the one I kept here to practice on, and my grandfather's set at my Flagstaff house. He was in the Marines when he was younger and played at clubs with his friends in Japan when he was stationed there. He died of prostate cancer right before I made it big. Sadly, there was no treatment for him as the cancer had advanced quickly. I was there when he finally passed and he told me never to give up on my dreams. My dad was diagnosed a year ago with the same cancer. Thankfully, his was treatable. Dad wanted me to go into his business, landscaping, but I was not the type of guy who had the patience to sift through dirt for hours on end and plant…stuff. I didn't even have plants because I had a brown thumb.

Music was my life and I couldn't see doing anything else.

I was right in the middle of tuning my snare when my doorbell rang. I jogged to the front door to find Rebel standing there.

"Hey." I moved back to let him in. "What's up? I thought I was going to see you this weekend." I eyed him carefully. "Why is your face swollen on one side?"

"Dentist. I hate the fucking dentist."

"Really? I fucking love the dentist. Bring on the needles and Novocaine!"

"Really?" Rebel's eyes widened.

"No, dumbass. No one likes the fucking dentist."

"Why does he feel the need to ask me questions when his fucking hands are in my mouth?"

"I know!" I laughed, then sobered and cocked a brow at Rebel. "You came over here knowing I have crabs?"

"From what I hear, once you treat them, that's it."

"Really?"

"They say to check in a week, but pretty much, yeah."

"You are a brave soul, my friend," I chuckled.

"What are a few crabs among friends? Besides, don't you have the NFL package?"

"Ah, so now we find out the *real* reason you're here." I laughed, walking into the living room.

"I was in town, so why not?" Rebel flopped onto the chaise end of my couch and crossed his legs at his ankles. "I saw Gareth last night."

"Yeah? How is our virtuoso?"

"I think he and Axel had just done the wild thing."

"What makes you say that?" I sat down opposite Rebel.

"Well, Gareth's already wild hair was wilder and Axel had a look of bliss."

"Really? It's so weird to think of Gareth pounding Axel. When he told me they were versatile, I almost spit out my drink."

"I know. I have a hard time imagining Axel on all fours, taking it from Gareth."

"There's a visual." My nose wrinkled. Some things you don't want to know about your best friends.

"You should have seen the look on Stan's face when that little tidbit of info came out," Rebel chuckled.

"How is Stan? I guess we'll see him Friday." Stan was still a little uncomfortable in his role as our new manager. I couldn't say I blamed him; he had to work with Axel against our childhood friend, Paul, to expose him as Gareth's stalker. I think Stan believes we hold ill will toward him, which we don't. He did what he had to do to protect Gareth. I watched Rebel carefully when I mentioned Stan. I was starting to notice little things whenever Stan's name was brought up. Rebel's lips lifted in a small smile.

"I think he's got a thing for me," Rebel admitted.

"Yeah? The long-haired, tattooed bad boy has an admirer?"

I had to admit, I *had* seen Stan checking out Rebel on more than one occasion.

"He's real shy, you know? I mean, I can feel his eyes on my ass when my back is to him and he stutters a lot when he has to talk to me."

"And? Can you see yourself on all fours for Stan?"

"Fuck no, dude. I'd be a top."

My mouth fell open. Rebel leaned over and lifted my chin, closing my mouth.

"I'm not opposed to dick, dude. Have I been with a guy? Nah, but I never say never." Rebel arched an inquisitive brow at the look on my face. "Seems you've been having your own thoughts."

"I don't know what it is. My mind has been wandering lately."

"Maybe you're sick of pussy."

"Maybe," I agreed absentmindedly.

"Okay, enough talk! Cardinals are playing."

I reclined on the couch as Rebel put the game on. I knew if I ever started dating a guy, the rest of the band wouldn't give a shit. We were friends with other bands in which all the members were gay. The more I thought about it, the more curious I became.

Rebel and I yelled at the TV for four hours as we watched our beloved Cardinals finally kicking some ass. We loved attending the home games; we had awesome seats. I made popcorn and Rebel and I reclined lazily as the game ended and the news came on.

"So, what is this shit that Stan is booking us on?" I asked curiously.

"No idea." Rebel shook his head. "Just said that we would get a ton of exposure."

"I hope it's not a Playgirl shoot," I snorted.

"You'd *better* hope it's not." Rebel pointed at my crotch. "You're naked down there."

"The worst part is the itching that's going to start when the hair begins growing back. There *is* a reason I don't shave anywhere."

"Maybe when you grow up, you'll have chest hair?"

"Fuck off. You staying over?"

"Yeah. I'm tired, dude."

"Well, I'm going to bed. Been a long day."

"Yep. Later."

I threw my clothes on a chair and crawled into bed. I was exhausted and I had no idea why. After my talk with Rebel, my curiosity was really revved up. Maybe I'd explore that side of myself soon.

~*~

Rebel left the next afternoon and I decided to head into town and rent some movies. I perused the aisles of the adult shop, keeping an eye out for other people. I had on my hat and sunglasses, but I was there to rent gay porn and really didn't want to explain that to fans. I snickered as I hit the gay porn aisle and read the movie names: Swallow Hal, The Sperminator, and Batman and Throbbin.

I picked up one that had gay guys tricking straight guys. Yeah, right, because straight guys would have allowed *that* to go to video. Confident I had enough to watch, I headed to the front counter and placed my selections down. The clerk eyed the movies, then looked at me. I coughed and nodded.

"That's it."

"Twenty bucks."

I handed over the money and grabbed my movies. I stopped on the way home and got pizza and beer and some of my favorite candy. I went directly to my room and put the first movie in the DVD player. I sat on the end of my bed, eating my pizza and sipping my beer. In the very first scene, some delicate blond was swimming in a pool and a huge hairy guy came out, dick wagging back and forth. Hairy guy jumped in the pool and grabbed the blond, smashing him into his chest and eating his mouth.

I was mesmerized. I could not look away as hairy guy threw blond guy over the side of the pool and licked his asshole. I wondered what that felt like. Would I like it? Fuck yeah I would, if the little blond's moans could be trusted. Hairy guy's dick was the size of a fucking anaconda and he shoved it right into blond dude's ass. Jesus, that looked hotter than hell and my dick was harder than steel in my jeans. I was actually turned on by this shit.

I needed to get laid.

I finished the first movie and put in the second one. Once again, I was hard in my jeans and this time, I decided to jack off while watching. I had a nice grip on my dick and was pumping away like a madman when my phone rang. I let it go to voicemail as my orgasm rose, setting off a bomb in my balls. I shot all over my hand and chest. I slumped over on the bed and exhaled. The phone rang again and I cursed. I grabbed it and hit 'talk.'

"Yeah?" I rasped.

"Get off your current fuck," Harley laughed.

"Damn, Harley. What's up?"

"Just checking in. How are your visitors?"

"Gone, ya ass."

"Awesome. Is that why you're fucking again?"

"I'm not fucking! I'm alleviating stress."

"Ah, jacking off. 'M-kay."

"So? What's up? And don't tell me nothing because I can hear it in your voice."

"Dude, I can't get laid to save my life! Achilles is on me *all* the time!"

I thought of the hulking bodyguard and grinned. Achilles was one of those guys you walked into walls for. He was no less than six-foot-five, blond, with icy gray eyes and a body most guys would kill for. He was huge and tatted and scared the shit out of most people.

"Maybe you should jump on that," I suggested.

"Are you serious? Achilles is not gay."

"How do you know?"

"I just do, K? I gotta run; I'm getting the stare-down."

"See you soon!"

Chapter 3

Jinx

On Friday, I was back in Flagstaff, crab-free and loving life. I jacked off five times in a row watching gay porn. I didn't think I had any jizz left. I pulled up to the brick building in downtown Flagstaff where we kept our offices. I spotted the cars belonging to Gareth, Ransom, and Harley, and Rebel's hog was parked off to the side. I opened the front door and sauntered in, grabbing some water on my way to Stan's office in the back. The guys were lounging around in the plush chairs that formed a U around Stan's desk. I plopped into Harley's lap and grinned.

"Get off." Harley shoved me.

"Nice to see you, Jinx," Stan said warmly.

"Ditto." I took the seat by the wall and crossed my legs at the ankles. Rebel shot me a grin and pointed to my crotch. I flipped him off.

"So." Stan cleared his throat. "I've been contacted by the producers of Singers, and they have two heavy metal finalists this year. They would like you guys to come out and play with whoever makes the cut."

"I love that show!" Gareth bounced up and down in his chair. "The British judge is such an ass!"

"He's not an ass. He's just brutally honest," I pointed out.

"Anyway," Stan cut in. "You guys leave Monday for California."

"I miss the beach," Harley mused absentmindedly.

"Well, Axel and Buster are leaving beforehand to scope out the venue. You guys have a choice — you can go by jet or by bus."

"Tour bus!" we cried in unison.

"Fine. Hammer and Achilles will accompany you on the bus. We'll be picking you up at 9 a.m., so make sure you let me know where you'll be." Stan paused for a moment and then smiled at us. "I know you guys will have fun."

"Monday at nine," I affirmed, standing up. "I'm going to go see my parents, unless there's anything else?"

Stan smiled. "Nope. Have fun and I'll see you guys on Monday."

~*~

I called Mom to let her know I was on my way. I stopped by my favorite coffee place on the way to my parents' house; it was the first place I went whenever I was in Flagstaff. I sipped my coffee as I turned down my parents' street. Things hadn't changed much since we'd moved in so long ago. I drove by the high school and frowned. Some of the worst and best years of my life happened there.

I pulled into the driveway of the house I grew up in and smiled. My parents had refused to leave it, even after I offered to buy them a new one. The house was still gray with white trim, the green grass in the front yard still mined with little plaster gnomes. I didn't know what it was with my mom and gnomes, but they seriously freaked me out. It was as if their eyes follow me.

Mom was one of my staunchest supporters when I decided to forgo college to play music fulltime. She taught me a lot about how to read music and play different instruments. She still teaches music at the high school, but I was her first student at home. She taught me to play piano, but my grandfather taught me the drums. I stepped inside and inhaled. It still smelled the same, like mac and cheese.

"Josiah?" Mom called from the kitchen.

"Yep, it's me."

My mother came out of the kitchen, wiping her hands on her apron. I was told I look like her, same hair color, same eyes; I guess I got everything else from my father. He was over six feet tall and built like a UFC fighter, even at fifty. I had to work out five times a week to keep my muscles. My mom smiled at me, rushing over to wrap me up in a hug.

"Look at you! My God, Josiah, you're so beautiful!"

"Ma," I sighed. "Please. Can't you call me Jinx? You did give me the name."

"It's your middle name, not your first name," she scowled at me. "And that is your father's fault."

I had to laugh. When I was born, they still hadn't come up with a name for me. While mulling it over, they both blurted out Josiah and then "jinxed" each other for saying the same thing at the same time. According to them, it came down to a close game of rock, paper, and scissors to make my middle name Jinx instead of some god-awful name my mother came up with. Dad won best out of three. And that was how I became Josiah Jinx Jett.

"I like Jinx, so you guys did a good job."

"Look at you." She caressed my cheek. "I always told you you'd be a handsome man."

"Yeah? Thank God I didn't stay an ugly kid."

"You were never ugly, Josiah!"

"Mom, please. I had acne, and I wasn't exactly thin."

"You're so talented, Josiah, and if those girls couldn't see you back then, they don't deserve to see you now."

"Thanks, Mom." I held her tightly. "Is that mac and cheese I smell?"

"Yes, I made it just how you like it."

"How did you know I was coming today?"

"I didn't, but you know your father loves the mac and cheese."

"He really does," I chuckled.

When I was growing up, we couldn't afford much, so we ate a lot of mac and cheese along with potatoes and that hamburger noodle stuff. To this day, I can't walk by one of those hamburger meals without wincing, but I still love the mac. Mom added stuff to it so it was never the same. The front door opened and I spotted Dad on the front steps kicking mud off his boots. He looked up and smiled when he saw me.

"There's my boy! Make me a grandpa yet?"

"I may have made you a grandpa a few times over, Pop," I joked. I got a slap to my head and winced.

"Josiah! You better respect women!" my mom shrieked.

"Mom." I rubbed my head.

"How's my supermodel?" My father waggled his brows at Mom.

"Okay, I'm going to the kitchen." I turned and almost ran there. My parents all mushy? No. Just…no.

"Josiah?"

"Yeah, Dad?"

"What's going on with you? Haven't heard from you since you came off tour."

My parents entered the kitchen holding hands and I made a face. Mom smiled and swatted my ass.

"Well, I just came from Stan's and he's booked us on Singers."

"Oh! You're going to be the band that plays with the finalist, right?" my mother guessed excitedly.

"That's the plan. We leave Monday."

"So soon?" She was clearly disappointed.

"Yes, but I'm sure I can get you guys tickets."

"We would love to come! Wouldn't we, honey?"

"You bet!"

~*~

We talked a lot as we ate, and my father asked me all about our tour. I'd sent them knick-knacks from each country we visited. Mom loved getting boxes. I think she just liked the UPS man, especially in the summer when he wears those sexy brown shorts.

There were pictures of me all over the house, from when I was a baby until now. My mother had a stack of magazines that I had been in on her china cabinet; some of them had pictures of me from back in the day. One day, I'm going to burn them. It was bad enough that *I* knew what I looked like; now everyone outside of Flagstaff knew too. The rest of the guys were always cute in some way, even when we were younger. Ransom got dates all the time; so did Harley and Rebel. I hung out with Paul a lot.

"Are you all right, Josiah?" my mother asked, taking my hand.

"Yes. I think I'll go see Paul while we're out in California."

"You miss him." Mom looked sympathetic.

"I do. I don't know if I should after what he did to Gareth. Shouldn't I be loyal to Gareth?"

"Gareth misses Paul too, even after what Paul did to him," my father pointed out. "Maybe he'll want to go."

"Maybe. I just don't want Gareth to think I'm not on his side."

"I'm sure Gareth knows you support him. And if you don't — well, his husband will step on you." Dad chuckled at the thought.

"He *is* huge." I nodded in agreement.

"They're adorable together." Mom smiled.

"He's a good man, that Axel," Dad added.

I stared at my father.

"What?" he asked, puzzled.

"Since when did you board the 'it's okay to be gay' train?"

"Son, I was knocking on death's door — it puts things into perspective. Did I think being gay was wrong? Yes. But I have known Gareth O'Donovan since the boy was in diapers, and he's a good kid."

I shook my head and smiled. It only took cancer to bring my father around.

"Now, about your old boxes in the attic," Mom steered the conversation away from the gay topic.

"I can't get them all now, but I can get them when I come back from Cali. That okay?"

"Yes, that's fine." She smoothed a piece of my hair away from my brow. "Eat up, I want to hear all about the tour!"

I helped clean up after dinner. Dad was in the living room watching TV, so I took a few minutes and headed to the attic to find a few of my boxes. I opened the lid on one and smiled. The box my grandfather made me sat right on top. It was wood, with a carving of a turtle on it. I opened it and fingered some of the rocks inside. My grandfather and I went rock hunting all the time. He gave me my first stone, a quartzite. Over the years, when he took me to different places, I'd pick up a special rock from each place. I used to always have the box with me; I guess that showed how much I had changed since I made it big. And not in a good way. I grabbed the wooden box and headed back downstairs. My mom put her arms around me and kissed my back.

"He's changed a lot, Josiah," she whispered. "He wanted to talk to you before you left on your tour."

"Well, he has time now," I argued.

"You know your father, he's stubborn."

"Most French people are," I snickered.

"You are French as well, Josiah," Mom pointed out.

"Shh, don't say that too loud."

"You could be named after your father," she giggled behind me.

"True. I do prefer Josiah to Josephe."

"Give him a chance."

"When he comes to me, I'll listen. How's that?"

"Good. I love you."

"Love you too."

Chapter 4

Jinx

I left my parents' house Saturday morning and drove back to Anthem to pack for California. I felt like I was constantly on the go, which I guess I was. I always looked forward to coming off a tour and settling at home, just lounging around in my sweats and vegetating in front of the TV.

The sun was setting and I needed to get out for a bit, maybe hit a club. I drove down to Phoenix and hit the main drag, windows rolled down, music blasting. The freeway was still bustling with cars as people were gearing up for a fun Saturday night. I pulled off one of the exits and parked at a convenience store. I grabbed my phone and Googled area gay bars. One popped up immediately with a five-star rating.

What the hell? Fuck it.

I pulled up in front of a club that had neon purple and pink lights flashing around — the fuck? An eggplant? Is that supposed to be some kind of phallic thing? Whatever. I strode to the front door and a bouncer in skin-tight, purple leather pants greeted me.

"Welcome to Dicks. I.D.?"

I handed it over and looked around nervously.

"Good to go, dude."

I pulled the bill of my cap lower as I entered the club. Patrons wearing white glowed eerily under the black lights, smoke filled the air and there were bodies in motion everywhere.

I found the bar and ordered a beer. The bartender poured one out of the tap and slid it across the wooden bar.

"Whatcha lookin' for? A quick roll? A quick suck?"

"Um, not sure," I mumbled.

"Well, I suggest the bathroom for starters. Get your feet a bit wet — so to speak."

"That bathroom?" I pointed to the one behind the bar.

"No, *that* bathroom." He pointed across from me.

"Okay." I downed my beer for courage and rose from the stool.

"Have a good time!" the bartender cackled as I crossed the club floor to the bathroom.

I opened the door a crack and peeked in. I heard moans of ecstasy and ventured in further. The two stalls on the end were open, and a blond-haired man walked into the one on the very end. I surveyed the bathroom quickly as I headed in the direction of the stall next to the one the man had just occupied. The moans around me died down as I shut the door and stared at the wall between the stalls. There was a hole carved in it, and an arrow drawn above it pointed down. I took a quick look around as I tried to figure out what I was going to do. The main bathroom door shut and then music filtered from the speakers above me. Nickelback's 'Figured You Out' began to play. Fitting, I supposed.

"You going to stick it through, or what?" The voice in the next stall made me jump.

"Um … yeah."

I unzipped my pants and took out my already hardening cock. Wordlessly, I thrust my dick into the hole and held my breath to see what would happen next. I'd heard about these things before, courtesy of Axel. I think they called them glory holes.

Moist heat moved across the head of my dick, and then a teasing tongue flicked at my rim. My hands went to the top of the stall and held on as the guy licked a path from shaft to tip in one long swipe. My legs began to shake as heat surrounded the head of my dick and slid down. My eyes rolled back into my skull as I got the best blowjob of my existence. And trust me — I've had a LOT of blowjobs. My body started rocking and a soft moan vibrated down my shaft. I sucked in a breath as teeth slightly grazed my rim, teasing and causing me to jerk again. The guy on the receiving end of my cock must have caught on because the next thing I knew, he was taking me faster and deeper.

My hips bucked into the wall helplessly as my fingers white-knuckled the top of the stall. My breath became ragged as the suction on my dick increased, relentlessly sucking the life force out of me. That fucking talented tongue explored my slit, licked down the side and wrapped around, then slid back up and took me down repeatedly. My toes fucking curled in my biker boots and I couldn't inhale enough air into my lungs. My whole body slapped against the wall then and the urge to come screaming was strong. My balls grew taut, the hair on my neck stood straight up and my head fell back.

"Fuck, fuck! I'm coming!" I shouted.

The moist heat left me instantly, replaced by a soft grip that took me beyond oblivion until I knew I *was* screaming. My hips jerked, balls emptying of everything, including my sanity. I slumped against the wall, nose pressed to the cold metal. My eyes closed as I tried to regulate my breathing. Jesus, I'd never been blown so well.

Do I thank them for that? What was procedure?

I tucked my dick back in and left the stall, not knowing if I should say thanks or what. I opened the door to the bathroom and then looked back. I really should wash my hands. I had no idea what else was on that wall. I let the door shut and crossed to the sinks. The stall next to the one I was in opened and a man walked out. His eyes met mine and widened.

"Oh, fuck me," he whispered.

In two seconds flat, I was back at the mall with that golden-haired hottie with the bubbled ass of fantasies. His clear, blue eyes were still fixated on me as I moved forward.

"I know you," I said stupidly.

"Oh my God! I thought … the door closed, so I thought … holy shit! I just sucked Jinx Jett's cock?"

"Could you not yell that?" I snapped. "I'm not … well, you know …"

"Gay?" he drawled. "Here's a tip — don't come to a gay club and stuff your cock into a glory hole!"

"It's Jayden, right? You're the guy from the mall?"

"You remember my name? Wait, okay, back up here for just a minute. Why are you here?"

"I was, um, curious?"

"Well, that's just great. Another guy 'curious' about gay men." Jayden lifted his fingers to indicate air quotes.

"I didn't know if I should stay or what. I mean, how does this work? Do I thank you for a fabulous blowjob? Tipping seems to cross a legal line …"

"You liked it?" Jayden gaped in astonishment.

"Like it?" I laughed. "Fuck yeah, I fucking *loved* it."

And just like that, Jayden was on me as if I was a piece of playground equipment. His legs wrapped around my hips and we smacked into the wall behind me. He attacked my mouth, his tongue pushing inside until I surrendered to him. A moan rumbled from his throat and I gripped his hips tightly, sucking on his tongue.

Damn, the guy could kiss, too. Was he good at everything? My dick was hard again as Jayden slid up and down my body, his mouth never leaving mine. His cock was just as hard as mine; I felt it as it rubbed up against my stomach. Should I grab it? I was kissing a dude and I was wondering if I should grab his cock? I think I left my brains, along with my load, in the stall.

I cracked one eye open to watch Jayden. Damn, but the guy was so fucking gorgeous! His little whimpers and mewls were turning me on even more and I wanted to fuck him against the wall. Sadly, the bathroom door opened and a guy walked in. I pushed Jayden off, panting.

"Take that somewhere else," the buzzkill said. "We got people waiting for this." He waved a hand toward the stalls.

I nodded and left the bathroom with Jayden right behind me. Well, now what? I'd never gotten a blowjob from a guy before, but I had to say, it was the best one I'd ever had. Maybe there was something to be said about guys on guys.

We knew what we liked.

I pushed past the people on the dance floor on my way out of the building. Hot Phoenix air hit me square in the face. I realized Jayden was still behind me as I got to my truck. I turned to look at him and he smiled.

"What?" I asked.

"I can't believe I just sucked your dick."

"I'm um, negative. You know, if that's why you didn't …"

"I may be horny, but I'm not stupid." Jayden cocked a brow at me. "But that's good info for next time."

"Next time?" I spluttered.

"You mean to tell me you don't want that again?" Jayden sidled up against me, cradled my dick in his hand and squeezed. "You have the prettiest dick I've ever seen. The pictures on the Internet do NOT do it justice."

"Great," I sighed.

"You seem awfully, I don't know, calm for someone who's never been with a guy."

"Sex is sex." I shrugged.

"Then come home with me."

I jerked and took a step back. With that one move, Jayden's features changed from excited to disappointed in a flash. I looked him over slowly from toes to head. The guy was sporting some serious wood and his lips were swollen, no doubt from blowing me. I grabbed the front of his shirt and pulled him into my arms.

"I'll go home with you, but I'm not taking a dick up my ass."

"Oh no, I want that bad boy in *my* ass," Jayden said huskily.

Oh fuck and hell yeah.

"I can follow you," I said. "How far are you?"

"How far are you?"

I thought about that for a second. Should I really take this guy to my personal space? What if he was a pyscho and tried to off me in my sleep? Or told a fan mag, or God forbid — took pictures? What did I actually know about him? Okay, so he gave spectacular head; wouldn't that look great on my tombstone? Jinx Jett, offed by mind-blowing blowjob.

"I'm not crazy," Jayden blurted out.

"See, people who say they are not crazy, *are* often crazy," I pointed out.

"Call one of your guys and tell them who you're with."

Oh hell, wouldn't that take some massive explaining? I eyed Jayden; I could take him in a fight if I had to. He wasn't small, maybe an inch or so shorter than me, but in his tight-fitting T-shirt, he was sporting some serious biceps.

Jayden grinned at me and produced a coin from his pocket. "Okay, how 'bout we flip for it? Heads you come to my house and suck my dick; tails I go to your house and you get my tail."

I nodded and Jayden threw the coin in the air. It landed on his palm, tails up.

"Follow me." I winked.

Jayden followed behind me in some snazzy car I didn't know how to pronounce. He obviously had money, maybe he was a dealer? Or some high-powered attorney? Who gave a shit? The guy could suck dick like a seasoned hooker. Okay, he was at least somewhat normal. I mean, he shopped at the mall. I wasn't making sense, probably because my brains were on the bathroom floor at Dick's.

I chuckled as I pulled onto my street with Jayden right behind me. My skin broke out in a fine sheen of sweat. What the fuck was I doing? I parked my truck in the garage and waited for Jayden to get out of his car. He was on his phone as he walked up to me.

"Yeah, I'm good. See you tomorrow," he promised as he hung up.

"Who was that?"

"Good friend of mine, he was wondering why I was driving to Anthem."

"And how does he know?"

Jayden showed me his phone. "We have an app that tells us where the other one is."

"So you stalk each other?"

"Kinda. It's more for security than anything else. You could be a serial killer."

"I highly doubt that. I'm a drummer, remember?"

"You're the hottest drummer I've ever seen."

"And on that note." I put my hand out, motioning to the house. "Come on in."

I opened the front door and seconds later, I was pinned to it. The shirt I was wearing was basically torn off my body and hot lips devoured mine. I grabbed a handful of that delicious fucking ass and squeezed. Jayden moaned in my mouth and I lifted him up, carrying him down the hall. We ran into the wall twice but finally tumbled into my room. I landed on top of Jayden on the bed and grabbed his cock.

"Oh fuck … yeah, squeeze it harder!" Jayden rumbled, pulling my pants down one-handed.

My fingers fumbled with his button, and then his zipper. The sound of it sliding along the teeth set my senses on fire. He pushed me off and shucked off his pants. I sat there with my mouth hanging open; he was commando. Soft, curly, manscaped blond hair dusted his balls and a patch at his groin was sculpted perfectly. I ran my fingers through it in appreciation.

"You like my hair?" Jayden practically purred.

"Fuck yeah, I like hair. Hate shaved shit."

"Um, you're shaved," Jayden pointed out.

"Long story."

"No time." Jayden pulled me back down on top of him. "Less talking, more kissing and hopefully soon, fucking."

I tensed at the word "fucking." I knew I shouldn't have. I basically invited this shit in. Jayden pulled back a bit, searching my eyes.

"Hey, we don't have to do this."

"One step at a time. Let me get used to this."

Jayden rolled me to my back in one swift movement and hovered above me, his knees on either side of my thighs. He bent down to my lips and smiled.

"Let me take care of you," he whispered.

I nodded. Fuck me, I couldn't speak as Jayden rubbed his cock against my abdomen. His dick was beautiful, just like he was. A head as smooth as silk feathered across my skin repeatedly, leaving a trail of precome. His tongue played at my lips. I tried to kiss him, but he'd pull back, teasing me again and again. I grabbed him at his nape and pulled him to my mouth.

"Stop fucking teasing me!"

"Okay." Jayden grinned.

The kiss nearly knocked me out. Jayden came at me with all guns blazing, kissing me like an animal that hadn't been fed in weeks. It was feral and passionate all at once. He ripped my boxers off and grabbed my dick. My back arched as his thumb spread precome around the head of my dick.

"I liked those boxers," I rasped.

"I. Don't. Fucking. Care," he mumbled, his mouth everywhere.

My balls drew up as Jayden dipped between my legs, laving my sac and rolling them in his mouth. My hands gripped the sheets and I bit my lip as he licked around the rim of my dick again.

"You seem like a top," I barely choked out between licks.

"Maybe I am, but you're not ready for that."

Jayden sucked my dick down his throat and I cried out helplessly. The sucking intensified and I started to see stars as Jayden bobbed up and down, up and down. It was crazy. I was going to come again.

"Stop!" I panted. "Can't...gonna..."

"Nope, not yet." Jayden sat up and stared down at me. "Lube? Condoms?"

I pointed to the side table. He leaned over and opened the drawer; he pulled out my cuffs and lifted a brow.

"Kinky. I like it. But not tonight."

Jayden threw the cuffs back in the drawer and opened the cap on the lube. He slicked three fingers, then turned around, straddling me backwards. His hand moved back to his ass, and he treated me to the sight of his fingers sliding in and out of his ass as he fingered himself.

"Oh my God," I whispered. "That is so fucking hot."

Jayden leaned over further, giving me a glorious view of his asshole, fingers still gliding in and out. He began letting out small moans as he pushed in further, writhing on his own fingers. I was actually getting jealous.

"You want this?" Jayden smiled over his shoulder at me.

"Yes. Now."

Jayden removed his fingers and bent over, placing his hands on my kneecaps; he looked over his shoulder with a wicked grin.

"Condom."

"Yep." I fumbled with the condom wrapper, my hand shaking as I tried to get the damn foil off. I finally sheathed my cock and waited, my hand tentatively holding his right hip.

"Put some more lube in my ass. It's been awhile." Jayden wiggled his perfect butt cheeks at me.

I slicked my fingers and inserted one slowly. Jayden's tight, hot ass sucked me in, and I gasped at the sensation of being in his body.

"Yeahhh … more! And move them in and out, push up further!"

I did and Jayden gasped, his body shuddering around my fingers. He shoved my hand away and grabbed my thigh, pulling me forward. I grabbed the shaft of my cock and pushed into his asshole, just barely breaching his body.

"Oh fuck!" Jayden choked. "More!"

I pushed in more, trying to go slow, but my whole body was screaming for me to thrust in hard and pound until I couldn't see. Jayden's ass swiveled around my dick and I grabbed his other hip, stilling him.

"Don't, I swear to God, I'll come right away if you keep doing that."

Jayden stopped and I let out a huge breath, trying to calm my raging dick. Even though I was wearing a condom, I felt every ridge, every pump of blood in every vessel of his ass. My fingers dug into his hips as I started again, pushing up one inch at a time, trying to hold back what I knew would be one hell of an orgasm. Jayden fisted his cock and began pushing back on me, impaling my dick further and further inside him.

"Stop fucking around and fuck me, Jinx!" he roared.

I knew I was going to leave bruises on his hips as I thrust into him hard. He made a choking noise and pushed back on me again as I thrust forward. I gripped him firmly as I steadily plowed into him until I sunk to the hilt, pulling out and thrusting back in harder and harder. In, out, in, out and all the while Jayden was pumping his cock like a wild man. He grabbed my wrist and my hips stopped pumping. I was afraid I'd hurt him, but then he started moving. He pushed down onto me harder and harder, slamming my dick into his ass. All I could do was lay there in awe, watching Jayden's asshole grip my dick, his perfect pink pucker stretching around my cock. It was so fucking awesome, I couldn't look away.

My balls grew tight and a tingle at the base of my spine began to spread throughout my whole body. My abs clenched as fire roared from my nutsack and blasted out my cock. My hips bucked and Jayden cried out as white streams of ejaculate hit my comforter before he collapsed over my legs. I slowly removed my dick from his body, and peeled off the condom. I threw it in the trashcan next to the bed. Jayden was still draped over my legs, breathing hard. I moved carefully, maneuvering out from under him. He plopped on the bed and breathed out a huge sigh. I leaned over and trailed kisses along his shoulders.

"Mmm, that feels good," Jayden mumbled.

"You okay? I didn't hurt you, did I?"

"Nope. You have one nice dick, Jinx Jett. I love the way it leans to the side just a bit. Feels great on my anal walls."

"I always thought it leaned because I jacked off so much as a kid."

Jayden chuckled. "Whatever you did, it's perfect. I love it."

"Yeah? You seem to enjoy giving head."

"I love the texture of your skin on my tongue, it just glides down my throat." Jayden sighed in bliss.

"Um, did you want to stay?"

"Is that your way of asking me to leave?" Jayden rose up on his elbow.

"I don't … well, nobody ever stays over but if you want —"

"It's cool." Jayden jumped off the bed.

"No, I really want you to stay."

"Yeah?" Jayden grinned. God, he had a great smile.

"Yeah."

"Cool. Can I use the bathroom?"

"Sure." I watched Jayden's ass as he crossed the room to the bathroom. It was perfectly rounded; the damn thing bounced when he walked. My mouth watered and Jayden stopped, looking over his shoulder.

"Like what you see?"

I nodded slowly.

Jayden chuckled and stepped into the bathroom, closing the door. I lay there on my back staring at the ceiling. I'd just had sex with a guy and it was the hottest sex I'd ever had. Why wasn't I freaking out? I knew why, but my mind hadn't gone there in a long time. The conversation with my father popped into my head. Now he was okay with the gay way? I shook my head. Jayden came back out and fell into bed with me. I rolled to my side and he did the same so we were looking at each other.

"Thanks for letting me stay." Jayden touched my bottom lip with his finger.

"Yeah, well, this is new for me."

"Well, your reputation was well-earned. You are fucking fantastic in bed."

"Thanks?" I smiled.

Jayden yawned and closed his eyes. I moved closer to him and put my arm around him.

"Is this okay?" I whispered.

"Yeah. I like it."

"Night."

"Goodnight, Jinx Jett."

I woke up alone and sat up in bed. I didn't see a note or anything. I checked the entire house, but there was no sign of Jayden. What the fuck? He left without saying *anything*? No phone number, no "thanks for the fuck," nothing.

"Well, hell."

Chapter 5

Jinx

The bus pulled up on Monday morning and I locked my door behind me. Gareth opened the bus door and grinned at me.

"Good morning, sweetheart!" he cooed.

"Ugh, don't call me that." I climbed onto the bus and grinned at the guys sprawled out on the couches. I'd spent Sunday moping around thinking about Jayden. I needed to relax and unwind with my buds. Gareth studied me intently and then sidled up beside me.

"What's wrong?" he asked in a hushed tone.

I shook my head, but Gareth wasn't having it. He dragged me to the back of the bus and pushed me down in one of the swiveling chairs. Hammer sat across from us, earbuds in, doing something on his tablet.

"Talk." Gareth pointed at me.

"I had sex Saturday night," I blurted out.

"Okay, that's not exactly 'stop the presses' stuff." Gareth raised his brows.

"It was with a guy."

"Hmmm. Still not major news."

Hammer chuckled and my head snapped toward him. He winked at me and went back to what he was doing. What the fuck? The guy never speaks but he winks? Gareth snapped his fingers in front of me and I turned back to him.

"What do you mean 'not major news'?" I asked curiously.

"Hello? You're talking to little Gareth O'Donovan, remember? I was at your house a million times as a kid. I remember your secret CD collection and your love of Lance Bass."

"Could you keep your voice down?" I leaned forward, trying to see the other guys up front.

"Whatever. What do you care what they think? They'll have your back, and you know it. You were my hero when I was a kid. You'd always talk to me about the guys and the newest album you got. Hell, you loaned me one of them. You always had time for me."

I stared at Gareth and he smiled. Damn, the kid had grown so much. I still couldn't believe he was married. It seemed surreal.

"It was because of you that I realized I wanted to have sex with Justin Timberlake," Gareth chuckled.

Hammer busted out laughing at that point and we both turned to stare at him. He shrugged his shoulders and grunted.

"Is your music even on?" I demanded.

He pulled one of his earbuds out and sure enough, music was blasting from it. He grunted again and went back to his tablet.

"Okay, weird." I shook my head.

"Look." Gareth moved across from me. "Whatever you do, you know the guys will back you. None of us care who you bang as long as you're safe about it."

"I used a condom," I assured him.

"Was he hot?" Gareth grinned, waggling his brows.

"You're not going to believe this, but it was the guy from the mall. Remember him?"

"Perky ass? Oh yeah, I remember that ass," Gareth snickered.

"His name is Jayden." I glared at Gareth.

"Oooh, already protective, huh? So, what happened?"

"He left Sunday morning. No note, no nothing."

"*And* he's smart." Gareth laughed.

"What's that supposed to mean?"

"I'm sure he knows your love-them-and-leave-them habit, so he did it first."

"Yeah? Well, I don't like it," I scowled.

"Getting a taste of your own medicine." Gareth took my hands in his. "Look, I know what you went through growing up. Ransom's told me a lot, but I saw first-hand how you were treated by girls when you were young. They're not all like that, though, Jinx. You can't treat them all like they're disposable just because a few of them fucked you over."

"You sound like my mother." I blew out a sigh.

"Thanks!" Gareth grinned.

"When did you, our baby boy, get so grown up?"

"Right about the time I was thrust into the limelight. I don't regret any of it, though. I would never have met Axel if none of this shit had ever happened."

Achilles walked past us, stopped, and stood in front of me.

"What?" I asked suspiciously.

Hammer coughed and Achilles glanced at him. A look passed between them and then Hammer lowered his head. Achilles pressed on his ear mic and began smiling.

"Oh come on!" I snapped. "Is he talking to you?"

Achilles squatted in front of me and tilted his head to one side.

"No one cares, Jinx."

My mouth fell open at the tone of his voice. It was so … soft. Who would have thunk it? Big, badass Achilles was soft-spoken. He stood, righted his shirt and went to the front of the bus.

"Jesus, that man is walking sex," Gareth mused.

Hammer snorted.

"Oh for fuck's sake! Stop pretending like you're not listening when it's obvious you are!" I pointed at him.

Gareth chuckled, placing his hand on my shoulder. "I'm here for ya. I think I always knew you were bisexual."

"You couldn't have said something?"

"Nope. Everyone comes to realize who they are in their own time. When you were younger, I don't think you associated the way you felt about Lance Bass as 'gay.' I think you just thought he was handsome and you wished you looked like him."

"Are you a shrink now?" I cocked a brow.

"Nah. I just read a lot." Gareth snuck a peek at Hammer. "Take Hammer, for instance. He's a very handsome man. Tall, dark, and scary, but under the surface, you can see that he's a very caring man. I also think he's Italian."

"He does look Italian, doesn't he?" I agreed.

Hammer turned his head slightly and cocked a brow.

"I also got the skinny on him from Axel. They call him hammer because that's what it feels like when he hits you."

"It's annoying, huh?" I glared at Hammer. "Having people talk about you while you're sitting right there."

Hammer shrugged and went back to his tablet.

"Ugh." I dragged my hands down my face and looked up at Gareth. "I also liked Kevin Richardson."

"Yep. I remember. He *was* hot. That black hair and blue eyes combo," Gareth sighed.

"I can't believe we're sitting here talking about guys," I chuckled.

"You think you're the only one of us who finds guys hot or who messed around? Um, hello? My brother and Paul?"

The subject of Paul changed my mood immediately. I wrung my hands and glanced at Gareth.

"Speaking of Paul, I was, um, hoping to go visit him when we're in Cali."

"Sure, you can ride with me."

"You're going?" I asked, my eyes wide.

"Look, whatever Paul did, he's still Paul. We grew up with him; he's been a part of all our lives. He's getting help, and that's all that matters. I actually talked to him on the phone when he was finally allowed calls."

"How'd that go?"

"Good actually. Axel wasn't happy about it; you know how he feels about Paul. He actually told Paul if he ever hurt me again, he'd bury him somewhere in Alaska."

"Ouch!"

"That man is so funny," Gareth beamed.

"Yeah, right. Funny."

It was hard to see little Gareth as a grown man, married to a former killer. Somewhere along the way, I'd missed out on Gareth coming into his own. He was sweet, caring, and obviously very forgiving. I spent a lot of time with him when he was a kid. Between the guys and the band, Gareth was around a lot. I mussed his hair and gave him a genuine smile.

"You're a good guy, Gareth."

"Yeah, well." Gareth struck a pose.

"We're stopping for gas!" Stan shouted from up front.

"Cool, I need some candy or something." Gareth stood and I took his hand.

"Hey, thanks for the talk."

"Do what makes you happy, Jinx."

Eight hours later, we pulled into the Hilton at Universal. I stepped off the bus and an eerie feeling passed through me. My life was about to change and I had no clue how.

Chapter 6

Jayden

"Sonofabitch!" I threw my phone across the room and paced.

"Something vexes thee?" Evander cocked an eyebrow at me.

"My parents refuse to send me my drum set until I see them. What is *wrong* with them? They basically told me to move out and take my gayness with me!"

"Hmm." Evander tapped his chin. "Could it be that you're in a band that is number one all over the world right now?"

"Oh, I'm sure it is," I sighed and plopped down on one of the chairs in the living room.

The Spiros twins, Dimos and Dimas were in a fight to the death playing "Halo" while Evander relaxed on the king-size bed reading a magazine. The producers of the reality show Singers had set us up in the Hilton at Universal Studios since we were the winners last season. They were winding down the second season and invited us back to play with the new winner. I looked forward to it, actually. Without the show, I wouldn't be where I was.

Although, right now I was beyond pissed because my parents didn't give me all my stuff when I sent movers to Alabama to get it all. They allowed them to pack up my room and that was it. The movers didn't know my drum set was in the basement. I didn't either, seeing as how my parents moved it there after I left. Now they were apparently holding my set hostage. They didn't want me in the house after I came out, but now that I was famous they wanted to see me?

Coincidence? I think not.

There were only two things in my life that meant the world to me — my drum set and my collection of crystal penguins. My grandmother loved penguins, and she left her collection to me when she passed away. When I left, I could only pack one crystal penguin and my penguin pebble. I was too afraid to take the rest of the set for fear they'd break.

I sighed and ran my hand through my hair. I loved my parents, right up until they kicked me out. Well, that wasn't true; I still loved them. I was just angry. I could almost understand their attitude toward me if they went to church and thought I was an abomination, but it had nothing to do with God. They just found it disgusting that I liked dick.

I snickered and Evander glanced over at me.

"Sorry. Memory Lane," I explained.

"So, what are you going to do?" Evander asked.

"I don't know. I can't think about that right now. We have to get our shit together and head down to the studio."

I stepped in front of the huge TV set and both Dimas and Dimos looked up, eyes glazed.

"Hey! I almost had him!" Dimas scowled at me.

"Yeah, right," I chuckled.

The twins were just that — twins. Their hairstyles were the only way I could tell them apart. Dimas kept his hair short, while Dimos' reached his shoulders. Both had black-as-night eyes with ridiculously long lashes. Evander, on the other hand, had dark brown hair with highlights. The four of us couldn't be more different, but we worked. I spent hours on end with these guys and they had become my family.

We left the room and headed down to catch a ride to the studio. I paced thinking about what I was going to do with Mom and Dad. I knew it was about money. I was one hundred percent sure of that. My parents weren't well off and this was their way of extracting what they think I owed them for the years of housing me. Funny how they stopped paying for my college right after I came out to them. I'd be lucky if I had time to go back.

The hired van came around the corner and stopped in front of us. Screams erupted behind us and I turned to see a handful of teenage girls running out of the hotel.

"Uh oh!" I laughed. "I think we're going to be late."

"Another round of girls thinking they can lure you to the vagina side." Evander elbowed me.

"Just smile and be nice." I elbowed him back.

The guys and I stood around signing posters, shirts and, sometimes, skin. The Spiros twins were covered in girls as Evander and I stood off to the side with our own little group. Finally, we waved goodbye and boarded the van. Dimos reclined in the seat and felt behind his back. He pulled out a thong and his nose wrinkled.

"Not underwear again." Dimas shook his head.

I laughed and looked out the window as the van maneuvered around Universal. I couldn't believe things had changed so fast for me. Eight months ago, I was living in roach-infested motels in California, standing in line for hours at a time just to get the chance to audition for Singers. I came to California with a little under a thousand dollars in my pocket, all earned mowing lawns around my neighborhood. I was going to make it big, come hell or high water. I played the drums and I had a great voice; together with Evander and the twins, we kicked major ass. We might "just be a boy band," but each of us played an instrument and we actually played them on all our recorded tracks. Once we hit it big, I couldn't see living in California full time; after staying in Phoenix, I made it my home.

The van pulled up in front of the studio and the twins jumped out first, followed by Evander and then myself. I trailed behind, my head still lost in my thoughts. Evander poked me in the ribs and I turned.

"What?"

"You seem different. Like you got your schlong sucked and a good fuck."

I smiled. I'd been trying to put that out of my head for two days. Jinx Jett fucked me! I'd heard he was fantastic in bed; boy, were they right. My ass tingled as I thought about Jinx pounding into me, the way he kissed and touched me. Just one taste of him on my tongue and I was addicted. My dick sprung to life in my jeans as I thought about it.

"Dude, we are in public." Evander stood in front of me.

"Stop," I chuckled, pushing him forward into the building.

"I gotta know! Who did you bang?"

I stopped walking and pointed at Evander. "You are sworn to secrecy."

Evander nodded and I began walking again.

"I was with Jinx Jett on Saturday night." Evander tripped and I grabbed his elbow before he fell. His mouth opened, then shut, then opened again. I ushered him into the bathroom and checked all the stalls. I felt like I was back in high school.

"You fucked him?" Evander's eyes were wide.

"That'd be a no. I was the catcher."

"Wow." Evander leaned against the wall. "I didn't think he was gay."

"I think he might be bi. I mean, it didn't really seem to faze him that he fucked a guy."

"Well, he's never really addressed that in interviews, either. I think the last interview he did with the band, the question was raised and he said, and I quote, 'Does it really matter?'" Evander smiled at me. "You like him."

"Um, yeah. Did you not get that when we saw him at the mall?"

"Well, he *is* hot." Evander shot me a wicked grin.

"It's not even how he looks. Have you seen his pictures when he was a kid? He was so adorable, even back then. Those pouty lips, those eyes." I sighed. "He's so damn talented, too."

"Yeah, you mentioned that in our radio interview," Evander laughed. "I think you spent the last five minutes of it talking about Jinx."

"Hey, they asked," I shrugged.

"We need to get to practice." Evander opened the bathroom door. He looked back at me. "So, no details about his dick?"

"No."

"A guy can try."

We met up with the twins in the studio just as our manager walked in. Sebastian Lowery was an intimidating man. As one of the judges on the show, what he said went. He towered over us, and I was six feet tall. Sebastian smiled at us as he sauntered in, a cloud of expensive cologne having already announced him.

"Boys." He nodded to us.

"Mr. Lowery," we all replied dutifully.

"Now, now. How many times have I told you to address me as Sebastian? I am your manager *and* your friend."

"So, what's up? Are we playing our current hit?" I asked.

"I think not. I believe you'll play the song that won you the competition. I think your fans will love it."

"Yes, the fans who don't understand why we're called London Boys when only one of us is British." Dimos chuckled.

"Evander is British enough for all of you." Sebastian winked.

"Bloody hell," Evander murmured.

"Sod off!" I laughed.

Dimas lifted a guitar up and slung the strap around his neck. "So what's the hush-hush all about around here? People are murmuring about a special guest?"

"That is a surprise best left for tomorrow. Jericho is probably going to win the competition."

"He's great!" I enthused. "His voice has a rasp to it that's awesome. He's perfect for heavy metal."

"Well, America appears to agree." Sebastian folded his arms. "The votes from the last show put him at the top. I do think that he and Zeke should win. If it were up to me, that is."

"Maybe you can put them together in a band?" I offered.

"I think Zeke knows he's close, but not close enough. He'll get a record deal either way. He's talented. Putting them together would be quite an investment."

"So do it. If anyone can pull it off, you can. I mean, look at us." I grabbed the guys around their shoulders. "We are SO in love!"

"So cute, Jayden. I do love you guys." Sebastian walked around the stage and peered out at the seats. "Your equipment is here, so set up and get some practice in. You have two weeks before the finale."

"Yes sir!" I walked around the drum set and sat down, picking up the sticks and twirling them.

"You have a few hours, use them wisely. I'll be back this evening to take you out to dinner."

"Later, Sebastian!" I called from behind the drums. I hit the hi-hat and Evander grabbed his guitar.

"Let's do this!" he shouted.

Evander faced me and I nodded. I closed my eyes and let the music flow through me. I picked up on the second verse.

Don't tell me you don't care
I can feel the heat in your stare
Come baby, come with me
Let's go for a ride, leave the world behind
Love when you touch me and kiss me slow
It's not over if you can't let go
Come baby, come with me
The words you say cut straight to my heart
Saying I'm sorry would be a good start
I thought it was love
I guess I was wrong
So I'll pour out my heart in the form of a song.

"Hold up!" Evander put his hand up.

"What?" I hated stopping in the middle of rehearsal. Especially in the middle of pouring my heart out in a song.

"I gotta pee."

I laughed and banged my head on my tom.

The rest of the day was spent practicing and fucking around. We all had strange ways of winding down when we fucked up. I concentrated on playing as the guys lolled around on the couch off to the side of the stage. My muscles ached as I played with complete concentration. I opened my eyes to see the guys staring at me.

"Jesus, I didn't know you could play that." Dimas stared at me, mouth agape.

"Yeah. I taught myself a long time ago," I admitted.

"You're talented, Jayden. I mean *really* talented."

"Thanks." I ducked my head.

Loud clapping startled me and Sebastian walked onto the stage.

"Very good, Jayden. I knew I was right when I picked you. Are you guys ready to eat?"

"I could eat." I nodded.

After eating day-old donuts and dollar meals when I first came to Los Angeles, every time I went out to eat, I felt like I was being spoiled. We followed Sebastian as we left the building. A stretch limo pulled up and we piled in. This life still hadn't completely registered with me. Some days, I woke up and thought I was back in Alabama. Okay, I don't HATE Alabama. There were some beautiful places there. I hated the nothing-to-do small town and small-minded parents that made my dreams impossible. The limo's heated leather seats warmed my ass and I stared at the mini bar overflowing with alcoholic beverages. I wasn't a big drinker, never had been. I wasn't the type who did drugs either.

"Bubba Gump's or Hard Rock?" Sebastian asked us.

"Bubba. I'm in the mood for seafood," I answered.

The rest of the guys agreed and we pulled up in front of the restaurant a few minutes later. I really wanted to explore the park and go on some rides. As if reading my thoughts, Sebastian spoke.

"You guys have a few free hours tomorrow, why don't you go check out Jurassic Park?"

"Yes!" Evander pumped his fist in the air.

I ate shrimp for dinner and gorged myself with steak, too. I had to remember I was part of a band now and I made a lot of money. I always put ten percent of my paycheck into savings. I thought it was probably a habit I'd never break. Scarlett O'Hara and "I'll never be hungry again!" and all that.

Sebastian took us back to the hotel and I hopped in the shower, washing the sweat from rehearsal off my body. My mind wandered to Jinx Jett as the steam enveloped me. What would it be like to fuck him? I knew what it felt like to get fucked by him — it felt fucking amazing! His lips, his eyes, his everything — and add what I knew about him? It all made him even sexier.

I'd tried to buy every magazine he's ever been in and the ones I couldn't get in a store, I found on eBay. I carried them in my backpack with me everywhere. Was I a little stalkerish? Maybe. But Jinx Jett was worth every damned dime. Never in a million years did I think I'd ever be so close to him, much less kiss him. My dick liked where my mind was wandering and perked up. I gripped it, sliding up and down while envisioning Jinx throwing me face down on a table and slamming his big dick into my ass. I came all over the shower tiles with a low moan, trying to stay quiet for my roommates. I cleaned up as best I could and toweled off, walking back toward my suite.

"I hope you rinsed the wall." Evander called from his room.

"Fuck off!"
"Ohhh —"
"Shut up, Evander."

Chapter 7

Jayden

In the morning, the guys and I were like little kids as we hit the park. I'd only been to California once before, and that was when my parents took me to Disneyland. This was so much better. We had the place to ourselves for a while before they opened it up to the public. Once that magical alone time ended, we were accosted by teenage girls for an hour, so we left.

Back at the studio, Evander and the guys took off to get water and I stood on stage, gazing into the seats. I was still a little nervous when I got onstage, but blinding lights helped because they obscured the people in the audience. Sebastian was setting up our first world tour and I was nervous as fuck about it.

"Hey, it's Jayden, right?"

I turned slowly to find Gareth Wolf standing behind me. His jeans hung low on his hips and he wore the band's T-shirt with the arms cut off and fringed on the bottom.

"Hey, Gareth. Yep, I'm Jayden Dempsey."

Right about then, it hit me what it meant that Gareth Wolf was standing there.

"Yo, Gareth."

My body reacted immediately to that sexy-as-sin voice and a shiver went down my spine and heat pooled in my gut. Jinx walked onstage and my dick popped up like that timer in a Butterball turkey that signals that it's done. His eyes met mine and widened a bit.

"Jayden? What are you doing here?"

"I'm in the show."

"Oh, are you a finalist? I didn't see you in the lineup."

"Nope. I'm last season's winner."

"Last season?" Jinx furrowed his brow. "I missed last season."

Evander and the guys came back, trailed by Sebastian, Jericho, and one of the other finalists whose name I couldn't remember no matter how many times I was reminded. Jericho winked at me and I smiled.

"Well!" Sebastian's voice boomed over the empty stage. "I see you guys are all getting to know one another. This is Jericho, our first heavy metal finalist, and this is Scott," Sebastian motioned to the other guy. "He's more of an alternative kind of guy. Gareth, where are the rest of your guys?"

"Right behind us," Gareth answered.

"Oooh, I sense some chemistry over there," Scott crooned. "Heavy metal is joining the boy band? I didn't know you liked them so … pretty, Jinx."

"Wait, what?" Jinx spun around.

"Oh yeah," Scott continued maliciously. "Jayden and his merry band of mates make up London Boys."

Jinx spun back to me, a look of absolute horror on his face. "You're in a boy band?" he almost whispered.

"Guilty." I held up my hands.

"You like 'em, huh, Jinx?" Scott leered.

I wanted to slap Scott in the face. No wonder I couldn't remember his name — it wasn't worth remembering. Jinx backed away from me and I took a step forward.

"Don't." Jinx lowered his voice so that I only I could hear him. "I can't believe you're in a fucking boy band! You guys barely sing, you just go na-na-na-naaaa, and you don't even play instruments!"

I recoiled as if I'd been the one slapped. Jinx was staring at me as if I were a serial killer. The anger boiled up and I lashed out.

"Fuck you, Jinx!" I stomped offstage, Evander hot on my heels.

I slumped into one of the dressing room chairs and covered my face with my hands. I was not going to cry over that asshole! So I was in a boy band. Big deal. Jinx acted as if I carried some sort of plague.

"I thought he liked you," Evander said softly.

"That makes two of us."

Gareth ran into the room and slid to a stop in front of my chair. He looked from me to Evander and held out his hand to Evander.

"Hi, I'm —"

"Gareth Wolf. I know." Evander shook Gareth's hand.

"Can I have a sec?" Gareth inclined his head toward me.

"Jayden?" Evander raised his brows.

"I'm good." I nodded. "Thanks, Evander."

Gareth waited until Evander was gone and then turned to me. He sighed, ran a hand through his hair and bit his bottom lip as if trying to decide what to say.

"I'm sorry about that out there," he finally managed.

"You shouldn't be the one apologizing. *You* weren't being an asshole."

Gareth took the chair next to me with a heavy sigh. He bit at his bottom lip again and then faced me.

"That was Jinx in survival mode. Whenever he thinks he's being made fun of, he's an asshole. He's got baggage that needs to be dropped off a cliff."

"Not really my problem, is it? I don't mean to sound like an ass — oh wait, yes, I do."

"He, um, told me about you two."

"He what?"

"He told me that you guys, you know, fucked."

"Well, I guess the secret is out," I said wryly.

"Look, I'd like to hang out while we're here. You up for it?" Gareth grinned. "You look about my age."

"I'm twenty-three."

"Cool! So maybe we could hit the park on a free day?"

I smiled. I couldn't help it. Gareth Wolf was one of those guys who you couldn't help but like. He was just so damned *genuine*. I couldn't fault him for Jinx's behavior. I was still hurt by that. How could Jinx treat me like that after the night we had together?

"Yeah, I'd like that." I gave Gareth a grin.

Jinx entered the room and I stiffened. He motioned to Gareth as he stood in front of me.

"Can I have a sec with Jayden, Gareth?"

"I don't think we have anything to say, Jinx." I stood quickly.

"Um, yeah, we do. How could you have not said anything to me?" Jinx pointed an accusing finger at me.

I slapped his finger away. "I don't have to explain a damn thing to you. Do you understand that, Jinx?"

"Instead, I'm blindsided in front of all those people with the fact that you're in a fucking *boy band*? What the fuck, Jayden?"

"Let me make this perfectly clear: I don't *owe you anything*, you got that? And I'm sure as hell not going to apologize for how I make my living. You stay on your side and I'll stay on mine."

"Jinx…" Gareth warned.

"Didn't I ask you to leave, Gareth?" Jinx snapped.

"Don't fucking tell him what to do! God, I was so stupid to think you were a nice guy!"

I pushed past Jinx and headed back to the stage. Scott gave me a grin and I flipped him off. Sebastian cocked a brow at me and I shrugged. The rest of the guys eventually joined us and I stood on the opposite side of the stage from Jinx. I refused to look at him. Thank God I didn't actually have to work with him; that exceptional privilege fell to Jericho and Zeke.

Sebastian talked with all of us about our schedule and what hours we'd be meeting. He handed out a sheet of paper with the times and details for the next two weeks. Once we were excused, I took off with Evander and the twins. We headed back to the hotel and I flopped onto the bed. I felt sick to my stomach and I blamed it on Jinx.

"Hey, we're headed out to eat, ya wanna come?" Evander poked his head in the room.

"Nah, I'll just get room service. Thanks, though."

Evander came in and sat on the end of my bed. He searched my features and a small smile played at his lips.

"You can always out him." He grinned wickedly.

"No. That's fucked up. I would never do that to someone. Don't worry, I'll get over this."

"Okay, if you change your mind or want us to bring you something back, just text me."

"Yup. Thanks."

Evander closed my door behind him and I stared at the ceiling. Sometimes I felt like I was in some other weird dimension. After growing up in small-town Alabama, California felt like an entirely different world. I seriously needed to think about doing college online or something. It sucked to think I put in all that time and did all the coursework just to let it go without getting my degree. I frowned, thinking about my parents' reaction to my news about being gay. I planned it really well, too. I told them I was failing economics; they were horrified. I thought being gay would pale in comparison. Yeah, I was wrong.

My parents were all about grades and saving face. They had friends they had to impress, I guessed. I kept quiet all through high school, just biding my time, knowing I'd go to college in Athens, Georgia, where people were a little more open-minded. I was right about that part. No one gave a fuck that I was gay in college. Well, that wasn't true. There were a few bigots, but nothing major.

When I told my parents, my father looked like he was about to hurl and my mother cried hysterically. Ridiculous, if you asked me.

So, I was gay. Whoopdeefuckendoo.

My mother had actually asked me if a girl had broken my heart and that was why I turned gay. Seriously? I had to explain that you don't 'turn' gay. You just were. You were born that way. I threw it back at her and asked her if a girl had broken her heart and that's why she turned to men.

That didn't go over well.

Out I went, with one suitcase and a thousand bucks in my wallet. One Greyhound ticket later, and I was standing in Hollywood with thousands of other hopefuls.

Waiting for a call-back was the worst part. Evander and I had formed a bond right away, and then the twins found us and that was it. We were inseparable. Sebastian was really good at seeing potential, and when he put us together, he'd hit upon another winner.

I ended up ordering a French dip sandwich with fries, hanging out on my bed, reading over my collection of magazines with Jinx Jett in them. I smiled at his middle school picture. Damn, he was so cute, even back then! Those chubby cheeks, pouty lips, and cool, gray eyes. He was kind of peering up at the camera and everything about his pose screamed "shy." I flipped the page to Jinx's junior year picture. He was the hottest guy I'd ever seen. I snickered at the name under his picture: Josiah Jett. I knew he hated being called that because he actually mentioned it in an interview. I loved the name Josiah. Maybe I would call him that for the rest of the time we were here. I snickered at the thought. I checked the time and yawned. I really needed to get some shut-eye. The rehearsals were going to be brutal. I just hoped America voted Scott off in the double elimination round.

~*~

I woke up to find Evander in my bed, carefully waving a coffee cup under my nose.

"Good morning, sleeping beauty!"

"Ugh. What time is it? And why are you so damn chipper? Did Scott get voted off the island?"

We all hated Scott, although none of us could remember his name up until yesterday. He was born with a silver spoon up his ass and hated gays. He also thought the world revolved around him and believed he was entitled to anything.

"Not yet! Let's be hopeful though, shall we? Now, drink your caffeine."

"You didn't answer my question. What time is it?"

"It's the ass crack of dawn."

I sat up, blew on the hot coffee and sipped it, groaning in appreciation.

"Get dressed." Evander smacked my ass and jumped off my bed.

"Can't I become human first? Let me finish my coffee."

I took a quick shower and walked out to find a tray with croissants, blueberry muffins, and scones. I grinned. Evander always made sure they brought me blueberry muffins. They were my favorite. He liked his scones and Earl Grey tea. He had to have both so he didn't miss home. His parents were both gone, leaving him a little bit of money. When he moved to California, Evander had tried out for several shows before finally trying out for Singers.

The rest was history.

Sebastian doted on all of us, but since he and Evander were both British, they had a special bond. The twins and I tried our hardest to imitate both Sebastian and Evander's accents, but we had been told we sounded too proper. Whatever that meant.

I pulled my sneakers on and pulled a sweater over my head, stuffing a muffin in my mouth as we left the room. The van was waiting for us as we exited the hotel, running right into Gareth Wolf and his husband, Axel Blaze. I had to look way up at the guy and he had a genuine smile on his face. He stuck his hand out to me and I clasped it, my hand disappearing in his huge one.

"Hey, Jayden, right?"

"Uh huh." I nodded, speechless. Gareth chuckled next to his husband and I looked over at him.

"Yeah, he's pretty intimidating, huh?" Gareth winked at me.

"You shut it, Munchkin." Axel nudged Gareth. He turned back to me with a grin. "Gareth says you guys are going to hang out?"

"Um…yeah? If that's okay?" I replied.

"Of course it is! I want my hubby to have some fun," Axel explained. "He needs some one on one time with someone his own age. You know, the rest of us are being fitted for dentures and replacement hips."

Gareth busted out laughing and I laughed nervously. "Okay."

"Seriously," Axel clapped me on my back and I stumbled forward from the force of it. I winced and Gareth gave me an apologetic smile.

"He doesn't know his own strength." Gareth took my hand and led me toward the van. "Stop breaking the singers, Lurch."

Axel spluttered behind us and I laughed as we got into the van. Three more men piled in and I swear to God, the van heaved out a groan. Gareth turned in the seat and motioned to the men behind us.

"Don't mind these guys, this is our muscle — Hammer, Buster, and Achilles. Guys, this is Jayden Dempsey of London Boys."

I got some grunts and then the large blond who looked like he ate guys like me for breakfast said hello. It was so soft I almost didn't hear it. Gareth chuckled and turned to face me.

"They don't talk much."

About then, Jinx, Harley, Ransom, and Rebel jumped in the van toward the back. Evander and the twins took the seats in front. I stared straight ahead, trying not to make any eye contact with Jinx. The van dropped us off in front of the studio and as I got out of the van, I turned to Gareth.

"You guys are staying at the same hotel?"

"Yep!"

We separated at the door and Gareth took my hand.

"Don't be afraid to call me or text, K?"

Gareth gave me his number and then waited for me to program it into my phone. I sent him a text and he grinned.

"Thanks! See ya soon!"

I turned around to find Axel right behind me. I looked up and tried to smile at the gargantuan man looming over me.

"Thanks for doing that," he said somewhat awkwardly.

"For doing what?"

"Gareth is surrounded by people older than him. He needs someone his own age to hang out with." Axel tilted his head in thought. "Although, Harley and Jinx act younger than Gareth does."

"If it helps, you look twenty-five."

Axel smiled and patted my back, carefully this time.

"Yep. I'm gonna like you." Axel walked into the building.

"So, you're Jayden."

I looked over my shoulder. Rebel Stryker stood behind me, grinning. He looked exactly what I thought a hard-core metal man should look like. Long hair, beard, and tattoos on every inch of his body. I couldn't grow hair on my face. Chest? No problem.

"Yes, I'm Jayden."

"Let's talk." Rebel put an arm around me and I swore I heard a growl behind us. "So, you sing?"

"I have been known to break out into song." I grinned.

"Play an instrument?"

There was a snort behind me and I knew it was Jinx. Sebastian walked out to where we were, saving me from answering any more questions.

"Hello, boys! Come on back."

We assembled onstage as Sebastian gave us our schedules for the day. The guys and I were going to practice vocals and a dance routine while Gareth and his guys used the instruments on stage. My back-up drums were set up on stage and at that moment, I wasn't sure I wanted Jinx to touch them. I glared as he walked around my set, running his hands across my skins. His fingers stroked my sticks softly and my body tingled as if he were touching me instead. Flashbacks of our time together played in my mind as Jinx sat on my stool and continued to tune my drums. His head tilted as he hit each skin, listening for just the right sound. I smiled as his expression turned to confusion, and then he flagged down Sebastian.

"Who tuned these?" he asked.

"Sebastian!" I called out before he could answer.

Sebastian headed over to me and I caught sight of Gareth standing over Jinx.

"What's wrong with them?" Gareth asked.

"Nothing," Jinx replied. "They sound perfect."

I grinned on the inside and Sebastian came to a stop in front of me.

"You guys get busy, eh?"

Evander, the twins, and I worked with a choreographer all day as we sang our number one hit. I was so out of shape. I was winded after three minutes, and the song is only four minutes long. I fell to the floor and rolled to my back, trying to inhale as much air as possible.

"We begin again tomorrow!" the choreographer barked.

"Ow," I moaned.

Evander fell next to me and wheezed.

"She's Satan," Evander groaned.

"I can't feel my legs," Dimas added.

"Hot tub?" I offered.

"Hell, yes."

"I need some tea with honey." Evander rubbed his throat.

"Me too," I agreed. "Maybe I'll just take the honey."

"Okay, hot tub and tea." Dimos stared at us. "As soon as I can move again."

Sebastian entered the room and smiled at all of us on the floor.

"Tired?"

"Yes. Please tell us we're done?" I pleaded.

"Yes, you are done. I'm having a party tomorrow at my house and you will come. We have a short day tomorrow if you want to go see Hollywood."

"Sounds good. I might be able to move by then." I attempted to laugh and held my stomach. "Ow."

"See you tomorrow, boys."

Sebastian left and Evander got up first, helping me up. We grabbed our stuff and headed out into the corridor. Jinx was walking with Scott, and I scowled.

"Well hello, Jayden," Scott leered again.

"Talentless pretty boy," Jinx muttered as I walked by him.

"Oh, that's rich coming from the poster boy for the STD of the week," I shot back.

"Ouch!" Evander laughed.

"Fuck you, Jayden!" Jinx barked.

"You wish." I winked.

"Jinx isn't even gay, fag," Scott chimed in.

I opened my mouth to retort, but Jinx moved like a predator, slamming Scott into the wall.

"Whoa, hold up a sec." He practically snarled in Scott's face. "Don't *ever* use that word around me, got it? You got a problem with gay people, that's your fucking issue, but Gareth is one of my closest friends."

"Dude, no harm, no foul!" Scott tried to inch away from Jinx.

I actually had to hide my grin. Scott looked petrified. I couldn't blame him, though; I'd seen Jinx's physique up close and very personal. The guy was built.

Jinx stomped off and Scott propped against the wall, his body shaking. I shook my head and followed the guys the down the hall.

"Well, that was fun!" Evander snickered. "I wonder if we could get them to wrestle in pudding."

"That's Jell-O," I snorted.

"Pudding, Jell-O, oil, any food group will do." Evander shrugged.

Chapter 8

Jayden

The four of us ended up by the pool, soaking in the hot tub. Every muscle hurt and my feet were excruciatingly sore. I closed my eyes in bliss as the jets massaged my back. Eyes open or closed, all I could see was Jinx kissing me, fucking me, touching me. It sucked that I couldn't bring myself to hate him. What was his deal with boy bands anyway? It took a lot of work to look this pretty. I chuckled to myself and groaned as my abs clenched.

"Dude, I am a prune. I'm headed up. You staying?" Evander grabbed a towel.

"Yesssss," I hissed.

"We're out too." Dimas mussed my wet hair. "Don't stay out too long and don't fall asleep!"

"Five minutes." I held up a hand. "I swear."

I reclined in the tub, my eyes closed in complete bliss. The sounds of the freeway were audible, but I shut them out, losing myself in thought. Jinx hadn't seemed like the guy I met at the mall, or the guy who had fucked my brains out. He seemed so sweet the night we were together. Where was *that* guy? Was he so rough and tough in public to portray an image of a rocker? Ugh, I had no idea what to think.

Footsteps sounded around the pool and I cracked open one eye. A guy was running in nothing but a Speedo. I sat up, wondering if I was seeing things. The guy hid behind the row of lounge chairs to the right of me and a few seconds later, another man walked out. He stopped and narrowed his eyes. The pool light was on, illuminating the area at least a little. I recognized him.

"Achilles?" I sat up further.

"You didn't happen to see a half-naked Harley run by, did you?"

"That was Harley?" I asked incredulously.

"Don't tell him where I am!" Harley whispered loudly.

I chuckled. I couldn't help it. A loud, frustrated sigh escaped Achilles and he advanced on the lounge chairs. Harley darted out and Achilles caught him easily.

"Let me go, ya big asshole!" Harley struggled in Achilles' grip.

"Okay." Achilles dropped Harley in the pool.

By this point, I was out of the hot tub and standing by the edge of the pool. A pissed off Harley broke the surface, spitting water.

"Dammit! It's cold! My buzz is gone!" Harley shouted.

"Get out of the pool, Harley," Achilles instructed quietly.

"Come and get me!" Harley crossed his arms with an exaggerated pout.

I covered my mouth with my hand to hide the fit of laughter I was having. Achilles turned to me with a raised brow.

"You want to join him?" he asked.

"Nope." I shook my head.

"If I have to come get you, Harley, it's going to be a long night." Achilles folded his arms across his chest and glared at a shivering Harley in the pool.

"Fine!" Harley swam to the stairs and wobbled out of the pool. Achilles strode over and grabbed a towel out of a nearby cabinet. He wrapped Harley up, rubbing his arms.

"There you are!" Jinx entered the pool area. He stopped mid-stride when he noticed me. "What are you doing out here?"

"I'm sorry, that's your business why?" I snapped.

Achilles looked from me to Jinx, and then to Harley. He put his arm around Harley's shoulders and began walking.

"Night, Jinx," Achilles said over his shoulder.

"Make sure he drinks water," Jinx called after them.

Achilles gave a thumbs up. Jinx turned to me and slowly eyed me from my toes to my head. I shivered as his eyes landed on my lips.

"Well, I'm going up. I'm cold," I announced.

"Wait, can I talk to you for a second?" Jinx took my hand.

My cold body immediately flooded with warmth. My dick, which had been tiny due to shrinkage, was now growing. I had to get away from Jinx Jett.

"I don't think we have anything to say to each other. You basically treated me like shit. In front of an audience, which makes it even more spectacular."

"I know and I'm sorry. I know I owe you an explanation, I just don't know how to put it into words."

"Look, I'm freezing, so can you just let me go?"

"I'll let you go if you let me talk to you."

I sighed and met his eyes. He really did look sorry, but what the fuck did I know? I nodded and Jinx fell into step with me as we left the pool area. I got on the elevator and my hand shook as I pushed my floor. Jinx pushed the floor right below mine and I gave him a look.

"I'm closer." He grinned.

"I need to change," I argued.

"Well, as luck would have it, I have clothes in my room."

"Jinx …" I warned.

"Come on. Please?"

"Fine," I muttered.

The door opened on his floor and I walked beside him down the hall. We came to the end and I looked down the hall.

"Are you sharing a room?"

"No, we all have our own rooms."

"Oh, we have attached suites."

Jinx swiped his card and the green light came on. A beep sounded and Jinx opened the door.

"After you."

I stepped into the room and wrapped my arms around myself. I was fucking freezing. My teeth began chattering and then a robe draped around my shoulders. Jinx stepped back from me and I slipped my arms in and tied the belt around my waist. Jinx sat down on the end of the king bed and patted the seat next to him.

"I'm good right here," I trembled.

"You're cold. Come here," Jinx invited huskily.

Damn that man! His voice reached into my swimsuit and stroked my dick. My pulse ratcheted up a notch and my ass actually clenched. In all my life, which wasn't a long time, but still, no one ever affected me the way Jinx Jett did.

"Can I get some clothes?"

"I like you in a robe." Jinx waggled his brows.

I started for the door and Jinx jumped up and grabbed my hand. He pushed me into the wall and gently pinned my hands above my head.

"Jinx …"

I gasped as his thigh insinuated itself between my legs, rubbing my balls.

"Yeah?" his breath caressed my lips.

"I … fuck … stop doing that," I panted.

"This?" Jinx raised his knee higher and rubbed my dick.

My God, my mouth actually started watering as Jinx leaned in closer to me, letting his tongue trail my bottom lip. I wanted to taste him so fucking bad my whole body hurt. I wanted him. I couldn't deny it.

"Fuck, you are sexy as sin," Jinx rumbled against my lips. "Love your lips, your eyes, even your fucking hair turns me on."

I clenched my eyes shut and tried to stay in control.

"Yeah? Even if I'm a talentless pretty boy?"

Jinx stiffened. He pulled back slowly and searched my eyes.

"I'm sorry I said that."

"Yeah? Why did you say it? What's your problem with me being in a boy band?"

Jinx sighed and let my hands go. He rubbed his hands down his face and exhaled slowly. I continued to speak because by that time, my word vomit had begun.

"*I* don't even like boy bands, but you know what? This is where I am and fuck it! I'm successful. Do you know I auditioned with one of your band's songs?" Jinx's gasp was very audible in the room. His eyes widened. "Yep, that's right. I sang *Manwhore*; the song fits you."

"I deserve that."

"Are you going to tell me what your problem is?" I placed my hands on my hips, glaring at him.

He just stared at me. I could tell he was fighting with himself on whether he should open up. He looked so damned good standing there in a black tank and sweats. I wanted to lick his skin. Well, my hands had minds of their own, because the next thing I knew, I had Jinx pinned to the wall and I had ripped his shirt off.

"What is *with* you and tearing my clothes?" Jinx gasped.

I flipped him to face the wall and then stopped. My mouth fell open and I gasped, almost choking.

"Oh. My. God. That is *beautiful!*"

Jinx's entire back was covered with a set of wings. It was so breathtaking, I couldn't stop staring.

"Thanks," he said softly.

It occurred to me that Jinx never showed his back off in pictures, and I hadn't seen his back the night that we fucked. I traced the feathers softly. They looked so real; like at any moment, the wings would spread and I would feel them across my face. I ran my hands down his back, his soft skin leaving heat across my palms.

"Jesus, you are so gorgeous, Jinx."

"Yeah, you say that now," Jinx snorted.

"What is that supposed to mean?"

"Nothing. It's nothing."

I flipped him around and stared into his eyes. He looked so raw just then, so vulnerable. I cupped his face, leaning in and brushing our lips together lightly. No matter what he had said or done, I couldn't seem to stay mad at him. Yep. I was a pussy pushover. Our tongues touched and I moaned as he took over the kiss, delving deep into my mouth and crushing me to his chest. He was so warm, his mouth, his hands, my whole body liquefied as Jinx wrapped his hands in my hair and the kiss became almost feral. I pushed him back and disengaged myself from his arms. He just stood there looking at me, his chest heaving.

"We can't do this until we settle some things."

"Like what?"

"Seriously? Let's start with how you've treated me."

"I said I was sorry about that."

"Yeah? Well, that's all well and good, but an explanation would be nice, too. You're okay with me behind closed doors, but not in public?"

"It's not like that," Jinx heaved a sigh.

"What is this, Jinx? Just another roll in the hay with a groupie? Because if that's it, just tell me. I'm a big boy."

"This coming from the guy who left without a note or anything." Jinx cocked a brow.

"Oh, so this is payback?"

"No! Jesus!" Jinx gripped his hair in his hands and growled. "Why does this have to be so damned complicated?"

"It doesn't," I said softly. "Either you want me or you don't."

Suddenly, I was off the floor and a roar reverberated around the room. I hit the bed and bounced and then Jinx was on me like a wild animal. The robe flew open and Jinx's hands were everywhere — between my thighs, cupping my nuts and fisting my dick. I dragged air through my nose as he feasted on my mouth. My bathing suit was off and then I was naked, with Jinx Jett on top of me. His dick stretched his sweats and I gripped the waistband, dragging them down. His dick rubbed against mine, the sweet friction making my eyes roll back into my head. My orgasm was right *there,* boiling in my balls and begging for release. Jinx gripped my dick and slowly jacked me off, kissing me in time with his hand.

"Ah…fuck! Fuck me, Jinx!" I practically shouted.

"Can't!" Jinx gasped between kisses. "Nothing here!"

"Faster, fuck…faster!"

My hips bucked, sending my dick through Jinx's capable fingers. One, two, three, and I was gone, almost screaming as my fucking nuts exploded, sending jets of cum all over my chest. Warmth spread across my stomach and I realized Jinx had come too. We both stayed there, exhausted and holding each other. I moved first, trying to get out from under him. Jinx took my hand as I got off the bed. I looked down at him; he was covered in sweat and still panting.

"Maybe someday," he whispered.

My brows furrowed as I tried to understand what he was telling me.

"But not tonight," he added.

I pulled the robe on and grabbed my swim trunks. I looked back as I got to the door.

"You want me for sex, that's fine — but if that's all it is," I took a deep breath, "then let this be it."

I walked through the door and let it slam shut behind me.

Chapter 9

Jinx

I woke up and rolled over. My stomach felt funny and I glanced down at my torso. Cum was encrusted all over me. I trudged to the bathroom and took a long, hot shower, the events of the previous night coming back to me. I'd had a few beers with Harley and then lost him somewhere in the hotel. Achilles finally found him by the pool and I went down to assist as necessary. Little did I know I'd find an entirely edible Jayden by the pool as well.

My dick swelled at the thought of Jayden in his swim trunks, all that creamy skin just waiting to be touched.

I got dressed and headed to the dining room for something to eat. Harley was at one of the tables, hand on his forehead, sipping coffee. I grabbed a plate of food from the buffet, along with some juice and coffee for myself, before joining him. Harley looked at me sideways with bloodshot eyes.

"Have fun?" I asked.

"No. Achilles put me in the shower and then stood at the foot of the bed until I went to sleep. Do you know how hard it is to go to sleep when you know someone's watching you?"

"He really has his hands full with you, doesn't he?" I chuckled.

"Look at him. Fresh as a fucking daisy. He looks like he's had eight hours of sleep!" Harley pointed to the table across the room where Achilles, Buster, and Hammer were eating.

"Harley, do you think you pull these stunts to get his attention?"

He snorted. "I've always done this shit. You know that. I can't help it if I'm a fun drunk." Harley sighed, sipping his coffee. "What about you? I saw the way you looked at Jayden last night. You come clean with him?"

"No. I don't know if I can. Sometimes even I don't understand my behavior."

"I think you need to see a shrink, or have it out with your father."

"Do you know he actually said he liked Axel? That he and Gareth were good together? Where was this man and his 'gay is okay' attitude before?"

"Not dying of cancer, Jinx." Harley took my hand. "Look, I know your father said some hurtful things to you in the past, but people change, especially when they've looked death in the face."

I gripped Harley's hand tighter and leaned in to hug him. If Jayden thought my tattoo was beautiful, wait until he got a load of Harley's.

"Life is short, Jinx," Harley whispered. "Don't let something good get away from you."

"I could say the same to you, Harley. Don't be afraid to go after what you want."

"I have to be strong. I have no time for love or a relationship in my life, you know that."

"You have to live too, Harley. Make room for someone other than your parents in your life."

Harley stood up and looked down on me sadly.

"Listen to yourself and take your own advice, before you lose Jayden for good."

I watched him walk away and noticed Achilles tracking him from across the room. Our eyes met and I smiled knowingly. Achilles turned back to Buster and Hammer. I chuckled. Oh yeah, our Trojan warrior might just have a thing for Harley, and vice versa, for that matter.

Gareth plopped down in the chair Harley had just vacated, scaring the shit out of me. He smiled and tilted his head at me.

"Long night?"

"You have no idea."

"Well, we'll put our time in today, but then I want to go shopping on Melrose Avenue."

"Are you going to pull a 'Pretty Woman'?"

"I don't think I can pull off the hooker outfit."

"I don't know. You've got some nice legs." I waggled my brows.

"I want to see the Chinese Theatre, too. See all the handprints and footprints of all the celebrities."

"I'm down for that."

"Cool. Ransom's coming too; I think he's in need of some fun." Gareth's phone beeped and he looked down at it with a grin.

"What's up?" I asked.

"Jayden texted me. He wants to know what I'm up to today."

"Do you have a crush?" I said it jokingly, but God help me, my stomach churned with jealousy. What the fuck was wrong with me? I wanted the guy, for once in my life; I could admit I wanted a man.

"No. He's got 'Jinx' stamped on his ass," Gareth snickered.

"Am I that obvious?"

Gareth planted his elbows on the table and regarded me seriously.

"Not to everyone, but I can see it. You both look at each other with this longing in your eyes. It's how Axel and I look at each other. It's as if I don't know who I was without him, ya know? He's that part of my puzzle that got tossed under the table or pushed under the rug by accident. Now he's here and I'm whole."

"Are you sure you're only twenty-three?"

"Yes, now tell me what you think when you look at Jayden."

Right then, Jayden walked into the dining room. He was with his bandmates and hadn't seen me yet. One of them said something to him and he laughed.

"It's like, when I look at him, the sun just came up and it's warming me from the inside out. When he talks, I feel as if it's a sound I've missed out on my whole life. That sound I've tried to find, tried to create — it's all in him." I realized I'd gone off into my own little world just staring at Jayden. My cheeks flushed and I grabbed my juice, trying to hide my smile.

"Now that's the Jinx I know." Gareth slapped my bicep.

"Huh?"

"God, I remember the poetry you used to write. Of course, with some tweaking on your part, we turned them into lyrics for the songs, but I remember reading it raw, before you turned it into something hard core and heavy." Gareth took my hand. "You're talented in so many ways, Jinx. Jayden needs to see that like the rest of us do."

"Yeah? I bet he'd look at me differently if he saw me back when I was a kid. The only reason why he wants me now is because I don't look the same. My hair isn't greasy, my acne is cleared up, and I've lost some weight and put on muscle."

"You really think Jayden is that shallow? I don't get that vibe from him."

"This is why I have the love-'em-and-leave-'em rule. I don't get close and I don't get hurt. I'm still *that* Jinx deep down, Gareth."

"I know you are, and I *like* that guy."

"Well, you're the only one. No one else liked deep, thoughtful, poetry-writing Jinx."

"Don't forget rock collecting, blueberry muffin baking Jinx."

I laughed. I really did like blueberry muffins. That was probably how I gained all that weight.

"Well, let's get this show on the road!" Gareth stood up and waved Jayden over.

"I'm out," I said quickly, nearly tipping my chair over as I got up to leave.

"Josiah Jett!" Gareth called after me.

I flipped him off and took the elevator to the main floor. I wasn't ready to deal with Jayden just yet. The van was waiting and I bumped right into Ransom on my way out.

"Dude, did you steal something?" Ransom eyed me suspiciously.

"No, why?"

"You look like you just committed a crime."

I was really bad at crime. I couldn't even steal a piece of gum from the store. That made me laugh and Ransom peered at me closely.

"Are you on drugs?"

Was Jayden considered a drug? I thought so. I was quickly becoming addicted to his scent — his touch.

"Not the kind you're thinking of." I elbowed him playfully.

"Well, let's hit the studio. Gareth wants to go out afterwards."

"I know, I heard."

The van pulled around and the door opened. Stan poked his head out and smiled at us.

"Hey, guys." He waved.

"Where have you been?" I asked.

"Meetings with the record label and I went to see Paul."

"How is he?" Ransom asked.

"Hoping to see you guys," Stan answered with a smile.

"We can't wait," I promised.

"Good. Now get going. I'm going to sleep for the rest of the day." Stan winked as he walked past us.

"That sounds good, huh?" I glanced at Ransom.

"Yeah, not gonna happen. Now, move it."

~*~

We spent the morning banging out our song. All of us were itching to get out, and I think Sebastian figured it out pretty quickly when Gareth started fucking up and playing Britney Spears. He let us go for the day and we all piled into the van that would take us to Hollywood. I sat in the back with Ransom, and Gareth sat next to Jayden in the front. I wanted to run my fingers through Jayden's hair, touch his face and kiss him. I couldn't stop thinking about him and that had *never* happened to me.

The van dropped us off in front of the Chinese Theatre and Gareth pulled out his phone, snapping pictures of all the stars on the walk. Jayden walked next to him, the two of them talking in hushed tones and laughing. I strolled behind them with Ransom, who also was taking pictures. Jayden was wearing form-fitting jeans this morning with a ratty pair of sneakers. How the guy managed to look like a model all the time was beyond me. I knew what I looked like now, but it still felt like I was acne-covered, overweight Josiah Jinx Jett. Falling for someone was not in the cards for me; I didn't think I could truly be myself without thinking someone was going to laugh in my face again.

Sebastian was throwing a party that evening in the Hollywood Hills and we were expected to dress nicely. Like I had a tux lying around. I snorted to myself and Ransom turned his attention to me.

"What's up?"

"We have to wear nice clothes tonight. Like I have a closetful of those."

"That's why we're here, remember? If I recall, you have a gorgeous gray suit you wear to events."

"I didn't bring it! Hell, I didn't know we were going to have to attend some swanky party."

"Well, now's your chance to Hollywood yourself." Ransom yanked me into a men's suit store and Gareth followed with Jayden. The sales clerk looked me over as Ransom perused the ties.

"Turn around please," the clerk instructed.

I did and heard a low whistle behind me. I peered over my shoulder to see Jayden licking his lips. In a nanosecond, I was hard as a rock. Those eyes lifted slowly, eyeing my backside until they met my eyes. Jayden winked and the sales clerk clucked his tongue.

"I have just the suit for you."

I stepped into the dressing room and waited for the clerk to return. He moved the curtain and handed me a navy suit. Shutting the curtain, I removed my clothing and tried it on. I turned and looked at my ass in the mirror. My cheeks stood out perfectly under the material. I turned to face the front and eyed my crotch.

"Yep. I'm Catholic," I snickered.

"Jinx?" Gareth peeked behind the curtain and his mouth fell open. "Damn, you could be a model!"

"Let me see!" Ransom opened the other side of the curtain and gasped. "Damn, Jinx!"

"Are you both done?" I knew my cheeks were red. I stepped out of the dressing room, over to the full-length mirror beside a row of suits. The sales clerk bustled around me, measuring my inseam and making sure the pants were at the right length at my ankle.

"Wow. Jinx … just wow."

I looked in the mirror to see Jayden behind me in his own suit. Fuck, God broke the mold on him. The suit was tailored just for him. Double-breasted pinstriped, with creases that accentuated his muscular thighs.

"Yeah, um, thanks."

"Would you like this one, sir? I can have it ready in a few minutes." The clerk was attentive, but not obsequious.

"Yes, please."

Ransom and Gareth walked out to model their own suits. The two didn't look a thing alike, but were both incredibly handsome in their own way.

"So? We ready for this party?" Gareth asked.

"Is Axel coming?" I asked.

"Yes, he's already got a suit, though, as do the rest of the bodyguards. They gotta fit in, ya know," Gareth replied.

Achilles in a suit? Couldn't wait to see Harley's reaction to that. Speaking of Harley…

"Where are Harley and Rebel?" I asked.

"At the salon," Ransom chuckled.

"Oh hell, Rebel's not getting a haircut, is he?"

"Nah, just getting a style, maybe a beard trim."

We bought our suits and left. As we hit the sidewalk, a bunch of women began screaming at us and within seconds, we were covered up. I signed autographs along with the rest of the guys. Some woman had me sign her right boob. I looked up to see Jayden glaring at me. I didn't know what to do at that point. I was Jinx Jett and I liked women, and it was a known fact. How was I supposed to reveal that I liked men? Well, one man. Jayden turned on his heel and walked to the van.

Chapter 10

Jinx

I didn't see Jayden again until the limo ride to Sebastian's mansion. It pulled up a steep hill and entered a circular drive. The two-story house was up on a hill, the back half on stilts looking over the city below. Sebastian met us at the front door dressed in a form-fitting suit, his hair styled and expensive cologne emanating from him.

"Welcome! Please come inside!" he beckoned us in.

We followed him up the stairs and I stopped at the top to enjoy the view. The room was completely glass-walled. Mocha-colored suede couches lined each wall, and a bar held center court in the middle. Twelve high-backed chairs surrounded the bar and coffee tables were placed in front of each set of couches. I walked to one of the floor-to-ceiling windows and gaped at the view of the city below.

"This is gorgeous, Sebastian," I fairly whispered in awe.

"I don't like feeling crowded, this affords me the feeling of being free."

"I can see that."

"Please, make yourself at home. The rest of the guests will be arriving soon!"

Ransom came up next to me, and gave a low whistle.

"Check out the view!"

"This is sick," I agreed.

More people began to arrive and I sought out Jayden in the crowded room. He was talking with Gareth, and

Axel was standing behind them, arms crossed and looking dangerous. Not sure he was fitting in. Harley was with Rebel, talking with the heavy metal finalist named Jericho. Achilles and the rest of the guys were hovering nearby.

Ransom suddenly gasped and I followed his line of sight. A dark-haired man walked into the room wearing a suit that hugged him in all the right places. Arctic blue eyes scanned the room before they landed on us. A smile tugged his cupid bow lips and he leaned into Sebastian's ear.

"Who is that?" I nudged Ransom.

"That's Sal Falco. Oh. My. God. Sal Falco is here."

I stared at the guy, trying to place him.

"Oh! That's the actor, right? The guy whose movies you treat like gold?"

"Shut up! They're walking this way!" Ransom hissed, suddenly looking panicked.

"Ah, Ransom Fox, I would like to introduce you to my dear friend, Sal Falco." Sebastian pushed Sal closer to Ransom and I grinned as he stiffened.

"What a pleasure, Ransom," Sal crooned. "I love your music."

"Wait, what?" Ransom stammered.

Jesus, I thought Ransom was going to melt into a pile of goo. I grabbed his elbow to steady him and Sebastian introduced me to Sal. I got a nod, a handshake, and a smile before Sal zeroed back in on Ransom. Judging by the sparks that flew from Sal as he stared at Ransom, the place was about to come down in a fiery blaze. By the way the guy was eye-sexing Ransom, I was fairly certain that he was gay.

"Can I offer you a drink, Ransom?" Sal motioned to the bar.

"Oh, um, I don't really drink." Ransom bit his bottom lip.

"Water, maybe?" Sal asked smoothly and I think Ransom groaned. Well, now. I think I figured out why Ransom never wanted Paul in *that* way. He had a thing for the dark-haired, sex-on-a-stick actor standing in front of us. I cleared my throat and leaned into Ransom.

"I'll just be over there." I pointed to the corner.

"Uh huh."

I excused myself to Sal and walked over to the other side of the room where a few women were hanging around. I recognized one of them, but couldn't put a name to the face. Why was I thinking tritons and fish? Her eyes met mine and widened. Arielle! That was her name.

"Jinx." She sidled up next to me. "I tried to talk to Harley, but he blew me off."

"Well, we are at a party. We need to mingle."

"How about you and I have some one on one?"

I looked around the room to see Scott the asshole contestant leering at me and jerking his chin toward Jayden. I looked back at Arielle and smiled. Jesus, you could use her tits as floatation devices.

"Let's take a walk."

We went downstairs to a large kitchen that took up one side of the lower level. On the other side was a long corridor, and at the very end, double doors. Arielle followed me as I headed that way. Four more doors lined both sides of the corridor as we finally made it to the double doors. I opened the door and Arielle gasped behind me. A canopied king-sized bed dominated the middle of the room. White silk flowed down around the bed and a large window filled one side of the room. The door shut behind me and I whirled around just in time to catch

Arielle as she jumped into my arms. Her lips gnawed at mine and I carefully removed her.

"Whoa, slow down there!"

"What's wrong, Jinx? Don't you want me?" Arielle unbuttoned her shirt and her boobs popped out. "You never said no before."

I should be turned on, I really should be, but the only person I could think of right then was Jayden. Arielle moved closer, grabbing my dick and rubbing herself against me. I tried to move back because, God help me, she was doing her damnedest and I wasn't getting hard. At all. I didn't want her and I really didn't want to be a dick about it. Arielle attacked my mouth again and I fought her off as best I could without actually hurting her. The door opened so hard it slammed the wall behind me and Jayden stood in the doorway with Achilles.

Oh fuck.

"I thought..." Jayden blinked and shook his head.

"Are you all right, Jinx?" Achilles asked sharply.

"I'm fine."

"Ma'am? Could you button your blouse, please?" Achilles addressed the woman with no expression on his face.

I walked around Arielle and approached Jayden. He backed up, still shaking his head.

"Jayden..." I reached out to him.

"No." Jayden lifted his chin. "Don't worry about it. I just wanted to make sure you were okay."

He turned and ran down the corridor and I started to follow, but Achilles gripped my bicep and held me back. Arielle walked past us, straightening her shirt.

"Maybe next time?" she cooed, completely oblivious.

No and just … no. God, was I so wrapped up in Jayden that I couldn't even function with women? Seemed that way.

Achilles dragged me into the corridor and shut the bedroom doors behind me. He turned to face me and I saw anger in those cool eyes.

"What?" I said in defiance. "This is who I am."

"Bullshit," he snapped. "It's who you *used* to be. Jayden was worried you'd been drugged or something so he came and found me."

My mouth dropped open in surprise. I'd never heard Achilles speak that forcefully. His brows were furrowed and his glare went right through me.

"Don't play with people's emotions, Jinx. That's not you," he continued.

"How the fuck do you know who I am?"

"I've been watching you. I know more than you think, Jinx. Jayden sees you, the *real* you, not the guy you show everyone else. Either let him go, or reel him in — but don't fuck with his head."

Achilles turned and strode down the corridor. Jesus, I'd never heard the man be so damn vocal — and he chose to try it out on me? What the fuck, man? I went back upstairs, but Jayden was nowhere to be found. Gareth shot me a look from across the room and I walked over to him.

"Where's Jayden?" I asked casually.

"He went back to the hotel. He looked hurt, Jinx."

"I can't help that," I shrugged.

Gareth punched me in the arm.

"Ow! What the fuck?" I pinned Gareth with a stunned look.

"Yes, you *can* help that. Stop being an asshole and own up. Grow up, too, while you're at it."

Seriously, was he really only twenty-three? "I'm going back to the hotel. I'll see you in the morning."

I went to Jayden's room when I got back to the hotel, but he wasn't there, or he wasn't answering the door. I went back to my own room and took a shower. My dick hung flaccid between my legs, probably upset that I couldn't find Jayden. I knew it wasn't heartbroken that I didn't fuck Arielle. I just … couldn't. Something about Jayden felt right, as if I belonged with him. Now, if I could just stop being a dick around him and be a fucking man, maybe I could be happy.

~*~

Morning came way too fast. I hurried to get dressed and grabbed my wallet off the nightstand. I ran down to the hotel lobby and into the gift shop. I grabbed a box of lubricated condoms and a pack of gum. The woman just smiled at me as I took my purchases. I stumbled into the dining room, hunting coffee like a lion stalking an antelope. But with a less bloody result. I also needed something to calm my rumbling stomach. The breakfast table held an array of foods, but the one I wanted wasn't there. I sighed and looked at the muffins on the oval plate.

"Who the fuck keeps eating the blueberry muffins?"

I ate some potatoes and scarfed down a bagel before jumping into the van for the studio. I was early, but I could hear music from the stage as I walked into the building. I crept around the corner and spotted Gareth playing *For Whom the Bell Tolls* by Metallica on his guitar and someone was hitting the skins like a fucking professional. I moved forward a bit and almost tripped as I spotted Jayden behind the drum set. Jesus, he looked absolutely beautiful. His blond hair hung in his eyes, sweat poured down his biceps, and his T-shirt was soaked.

It was the most gorgeous vision I'd ever had.

One of Jayden's other bandmates, Dimos, was playing the bass. I stood rooted to the spot, totally in awe of Jayden's ability.

Out of the corner of my eye, I noticed Scott Stupid advancing toward the stage from the seats. He already had a smirk on his face that made me want to slap the taste out of his mouth. Jayden began singing and I almost pissed myself. Damn! The guy had a voice! He sounded almost like Ransom.

"Impressive."

I jumped sky high and spun around to see Rebel head banging behind me with Harley and Ransom.

"Thank God he just stands there and sings 'na-na-na-naaa,' huh? Otherwise, he could give us a run for our money," Ransom chuckled.

"Shut up! I didn't know!" I whispered.

"Hey! Who's over there?" Gareth called out.

"Just us!" Ransom answered, shoving me onto the main stage.

Jayden wiped his forehead with his forearm and stared at me. Scott was leaning against the first row of seats, just watching us and I knew my inner dick was about to emerge. I tried so hard to stop it from coming.

"Make sure you clean those when you're done." I pointed to the drum set.

"Of course. They're mine," Jayden shot back.

"W-what?" I stammered.

"Yeah, mine." Jayden grinned wickedly.

"That was just a fluke, right, Jayden?" Scott taunted from the front row. "Bet that's the only song you can play."

Jayden twirled a stick in his fingers and grinned at Gareth. "Hey, Ahab, wanna back me up?"

"No way!" I shouted in disbelief.

"Way!" Jayden winked.

"Who the fuck is Ahab?" Scott asked, totally confused.

"Dude, that's Led Zeppelin's *Moby Dick*! Haven't you ever heard the drum solo?"

"Who is Led Zeppelin?"

"Dude, leave before I kill you for even asking that question." Rebel leaned in to Scott's face.

The guys and I took a seat in the front row as Jayden and Gareth began to play. My hands moved with Jayden's, almost as if we were both playing. It took a good ten minutes before Jayden stopped and he looked up. Rebel stood clapping, and Harley and Ransom joined him. I couldn't help it. I stood up too. I clapped for the guy who turned me upside down and turned me on beyond belief.

"And now a special song for you." Jayden stared right at me. He motioned for Gareth and leaned into his ear when he got close. Dimos leaned in as well and they both grinned.

Gareth came to stand at the front of the stage and leaned into the microphone.

"Some Nickelback for ya."

The music started and Jayden sang. I frowned as *Figured You Out* blasted across the seats.

"Well now, that's telling." Rebel chuckled.

"Shut up."

Jayden could sing and play drums. I meant, I could too — but I had no idea he was so amazing.

The guys finished up and once again got a standing ovation. Scott snickered at my right and I glanced over at him and sent him a death glare. Jayden came out from behind the drums and bowed with Gareth and his other bandmate.

"Thanks to Dimos for helping out."

"My pleasure," Dimos replied.

I jumped up on stage and took Jayden by the hand. He pulled back from me and I tried again to take his hand.

"Don't touch me."

"Will you let me explain Arielle, please?"

"Arielle? Seriously? Don't bother. I know how you operate, Jinx. That's how you keep getting fucked up with some STD. I'm surprised your dick hasn't fallen off!"

"Nothing happened!"

"Really? I could swear her tongue was down your throat." Jayden took a deep breath and exhaled slowly. "You don't owe me any explanations."

"You're right, I don't, but I want to explain nonetheless."

"Whatever, Jinx."

"Are you going to listen to me or not?"

"Not." Jayden placed his sticks in my hand and walked off.

"Jayden Dempsey!" I barked. "You owe me!"

He spun around, his gaze nearly scorching me from the inside.

"I owe you? How many have you slept with, Jinx? It seems to me you've done the walk of shame nearly every tour *and* in between!"

I narrowed my eyes and fixed him with a look. "It's

not the walk of shame, it's the 'just got laid parade'."

Right about that time, I realized we had an audience. In my peripheral vision, I caught sight of Gareth and the guys, mouths hanging open in shock. Jayden made some kind of spluttering noise before he stomped backstage. I turned to my guys and waited.

"Na-na-na-naaa," they sang in perfect harmony.

"Oh, fuck off."

Chapter 11

Jinx

I ran after Jayden. His footsteps echoed down the hall as I pursued him. I grabbed his forearm and spun him around. I hauled him into my arms and just held him close to me. Jayden sniffled and I nuzzled his ear.

"I'm sorry," I whispered. "I don't know why I do the things I do."

"Yes you do. You just won't tell me."

"I didn't do anything with Arielle."

"Yeah right!" Jayden pushed me off. "I saw her tits for fuck's sake! Talk about owing someone — you owe me for a sight I'll never unsee, an image burned upon my retinas."

"I didn't initiate anything, I swear it!"

"Yeah, okay. Fine. Just leave me alone, Jinx."

I tugged his arm and hauled him into the nearest room, which happened to be a janitorial closet. The automatic light immediately flicked on. I slammed the door shut and pushed him up against it, taking his mouth in a passionate kiss. Jayden fought me, his balled fists hitting me anywhere he could reach. He bit my lip and I gasped, pulling away. I ran my finger over my lip and tasted blood.

"You bit me!"

"I don't want this!"

"You came after me last night because you were jealous. Admit it."

"No! I thought you were in trouble, like maybe she had slipped something into your drink!"

"Bullshit!" I coughed into my hand. "You were jealous! Just say it!"

"Fuck you, Jinx!"

"Not right now, but maybe later."

I kissed Jayden again, making sure I investigated every single inch of his mouth slowly. I pulled back just a smidge, leaving soft kisses on his lips.

"I hate you," Jayden whimpered.

"Yeah? I hate you, too."

I flipped Jayden around so his ass was against me and yanked the button off his jeans. I slipped my hand inside his pants, gripping his rock-hard erection. He moaned, writhing against me. Silken skin drifted along my palm and I rubbed the rim of his prick with my thumb. Jayden pushed back against me, his ass rubbing deliciously against my denim-covered dick. I kissed his neck and bit at the skin on his shoulder.

"This doesn't mean anything, Jinx," Jayden rasped.

"It does to me." I pushed my hips into his ass. "I want this again. Can't stop thinking about it. How you respond to me, the noises you make, your skin on mine. I want to be buried in your ass."

"If you're going to talk like that, you better back that shit up."

"I have a condom."

Jayden stiffened for a brief second before his muscles relaxed and his shoulders slumped.

"Do it."

"No. I want you to want it. Don't act like this is a hardship on your part."

"Don't be an egotistical shithead."

I chuckled, licking up the side of his neck and nipping at his ear.

"I want this so much so, my dick is fucking leaking just thinking about being balls-deep in that luscious ass of yours."

"God, that's so romantic," Jayden said wryly.

"I'll work on my poetry."

I shoved his pants down around his ankles and yanked mine down past my ass. I grabbed the condom out of my wallet and sheathed my already hard and crying cock. Jayden kicked one of his pants legs off from around his ankles and spread his legs out, tipping his ass back toward me. I was momentarily frozen, staring at Jayden's exposed ass. My hands wandered over the smooth flesh, pulling his ass cheeks apart and staring at the puckered hole.

"Jinx!" Jayden wiggled his ass.

I lined up with his hole and pushed in. Jayden sucked in a breath and his fingers dug into the door. My hands gripped his hips, pulling him back onto me, my eyes closed as I relished the feel of his ass gripping me. Jesus, I couldn't even imagine what it would feel like to fuck him bare. He was hot, slick, and smooth, massaging my dick as I fed myself into him inch by inch.

"Fuck yes, Jayden," I choked out. "Feels so fucking good."

"Damn slanted prick," Jayden rasped.

"Jack off. I wanna see."

"Harder!"

My fingers gripped more tightly as I pounded into him, watching as my dick slid in and out of his ass was about to push me over the edge. Jayden was fisting his dick, one hand on the door, his hair in his eyes. Fuck! He looked so damn sexy just then. My breathing was becoming labored as I worked Jayden's hole, his ass gripping me, yanking me into that tight heat. I wrapped an arm around his waist and slammed into him. A cry bounced off the closet walls and Jayden came all over the door. My body jerked and then I was shouting through my orgasm. I slumped over Jayden's back and closed my eyes.

"Holy shit." I lifted off of him and removed the condom. Jayden stood up and turned to face me. His hair was slicked back with sweat and his bottom lip had a tiny dot of blood on it.

"Shit!" I touched his lip. "Are you okay? Did I hurt you?"

"I'm okay, a little more lube would have helped."

"Shit. Fuck." I shook my head. "I'm so sorry."

Jayden pulled his jeans back up and fastened them with a shaky hand. I covered it with my own and searched his eyes. What I saw there made my heart sink. Jayden looked devastated.

"What is it?" I asked worriedly.

"I can't do this," he whispered brokenly.

"What? You can't do what?"

"I know who you are, Jinx. I can't keep doing this to myself. I want so much more from you, but I'm not going to get it. You treat me like shit and I keep coming back for more. That isn't me. I swore I'd never let anyone walk all over me and I'm not going to start now. I'm not going to be another notch on your bedpost or check in your black book. I'm glad I could help in your sexual exploration, but we both know this just isn't going to work. I'm not going to hide out in a closet — literally — when I blew the door off my own."

"Look, it's not like that —"

"But it is," Jayden opened the door. "You can't be with me in public, and you make fun of what I do. I'm not feeling a lot of respect from you and guess what? I'm the kind of person who needs respect. Who *deserves* respect." Jayden stepped out of the closet. "Goodbye to this part of being together, Jinx."

The door closed and I felt as if I'd just lost everything. I banged my head on the wall and let out a frustrated shout. What the fuck was wrong with me? I cared about Jayden, more than I had ever cared for anyone aside from the guys and my parents. Jayden was … Jesus, the guy was smart, funny, gorgeous, and talented as fuck. And the way he played the drums? Damn, I was getting a boner just thinking about Jayden behind the set. I balled my fists and stepped out of the closet. Well, I was going to have to prove to Jayden that I wanted him enough to be what he needed, and I was going to start by facing all the shit in my life that I had swept under a rug.

~*~

The next few days, Jayden stayed away from me and hung out with Gareth. I couldn't blame him. I did what I had to do for the show and stayed with Harley a lot. I met with a few of the other acts that were probably going to be gone by the time the finale rolled around. Scott Stupid stayed away from me as well. He tried to talk to me once and I essentially growled at him. Then I sicced Buster on him. It was so nice to have big, burly, scary bodyguards on hand. We were taping live tonight for the double elimination round and the guys and I were dressed in our usual touring attire: ratty jeans and our band's shirt. I had my signature biker boots on and the makeup lady was slathering my face in cover-up.

"You have beautiful skin, Mr. Jett," she said sincerely as she smeared concealer under my eyes.

"Thank you." Sure I did. *Now.*

"Don't forget the blush on his cheekbones," Harley chuckled.

"Five minutes, guys!" Stan shouted.

Gareth leaned over the back of my chair and smiled at our reflections. "You look so pretty."

"So do you, Munchkin."

Gareth frowned and I laughed.

"Let's go!" Sebastian walked through the room. "Up, up! We have somewhere to be!" He clapped his hands as he exited the room on the other side.

I stood up and teased the front of my hair a bit. I turned and regarded all the guys. "Ready?"

We were going to play our number one hit from our last album, Blood, Sweat and Fear. Then, whoever won, we'd be playing with them. I was still a little shy on stage. Thankfully, I was the drummer and could hide behind the set. Sort of.

We walked on stage to screams and cheers. The five of us bowed and then got ready. Sebastian introduced us to more screaming and shouting and then Gareth looked over his shoulder at me. I hit my sticks together and we rocked the damn house. I spotted Jayden's guys right in the front row, but no Jayden. As we finished, the crowd went crazy. I jogged up to the front of the stage and bowed with the guys. Sebastian walked out and shook our hands. He turned to the cameras.

"All right! Start voting now! The window is open for twelve hours, so get your Tweets in and don't forget to vote on our official page!"

The finalists lined up on stage as Sebastian introduced them. Jericho and Zeke got the loudest applause, along with cheers and whistles. I crossed the stage and headed behind the curtains. Jayden's guys were walking toward the dressing rooms and I caught up to them.

"Hey, where's Jayden?" I asked one of them.

"He's not here," a dark-haired guy answered.

"I got that," I said in exasperation. "Do you know where he is?"

"Nope."

They all began walking again.

"That's a lie. I know you have that stalking app!"

The brown-haired guy turned around and stared at me. "How do you know?"

"Ah, must have been talking to you that night." I grinned.

"He doesn't want to see you," he answered.

"Evander, right?" The guy jerked a nod and I approached him carefully. "I need to talk to him. I have to explain."

"Explain what? That you want to hide him? That he's not a real musician because he plays in a boy band? Please, explain to me what you need to tell him."

"Wow, protective much?" I narrowed my eyes at the guy. "You got a thing for Jayden?"

"You're not helping your cause right now," Evander snapped.

"Fine!" I threw my hands up in defeat. "Please tell me where he is?"

Evander scowled, but removed his phone from his pocket. He touched the screen and then threw a glance my way. "I swear to God, if you hurt him..."

"I won't."

"Fine. Santa Monica Pier."

~*~

I took a cab to the pier and made sure the driver broke a few speed limits along the way. I needed to talk to Jayden. My phone beeped with a message from Stan. We were being given a few days off before we had to be back. I exhaled and smiled. We'd been working twelve-hour days for the last three, making sure we had everything down. Sometimes too much practice hurt, at least for me it did.

The cab dropped me off at the pier and I scanned the crowd for Jayden. The smell of the ocean drifted up my nostrils and I breathed in deeply. I had lived in Arizona my whole life, so beaches? Not so much in the desert. I skirted around a few fishermen trying to make a catch and caught sight of the bait shop at the end of the pier. A row of benches sat alongside the sides of the pier with lamps above them. Someone with blond hair was sitting on one of them with a magazine in his lap.

"Jayden?" I called out as I approached.

His head lifted and he quickly stuffed the magazine into a backpack and stood up.

"How did you find me?" he asked.

"Stalker app."

"Fuck." Jayden threaded his fingers into his hair.

"I need to talk to you. I want to explain, so please let me."

"Fine." Jayden slumped back onto the bench and stared out at the ocean.

"I wasn't exactly cute when I was growing up. I had acne and for some reason, my hair was always greasy. I ate too many blueberry muffins and too much mac and cheese and I was painfully shy. I couldn't get a girl to talk to me, much less go out with me. The one time I got up the nerve to ask a girl out, she laughed in my face. Now I have chicks begging to fuck me and I treat them like shit because deep down, I'm pissed at the whole female population. They didn't want me then, but a good shampoo, acne medication, and working out changes all of that? Suddenly, I'm okay to be seen with? So, yeah — I became superficial, and I treat people like shit instead of getting close to them because I don't want to get laughed at again. There's more, which really has to do with my relationship with my father. But the biggest reason I pull away is because I don't want you to want me for how I am now. I want to believe I was worth wanting and loving before."

Jayden stood up slowly and turned to face me. His eyes were so wide I thought they might fall out of his skull. He reached into the pack and pulled out the magazine. It shook in his hand, and I knew I was looking at someone enraged. Why he was so angry, I didn't know.

"You think I want you just because you're hot?" Jayden shook his head. "Did you ever stop to think just once that maybe I respect you as a musician? That maybe there's more to you than looks?"

Jayden threw the magazine at me. It landed face up at my feet.

"*That's* the Jinx I want. The one who collected rocks with his grandfather, the one who loves mac and cheese, the one who writes poetry and spends every single Mother's Day with his mom. That's the one! The guy with the greasy hair and acne who was a bit overweight was the guy I wanted! Not the pompous asshole in front of me now! I wanted you *before* I even saw what you look like now! The first time I Googled you, your high school picture was the first one I saw, and that was it for me. Your eyes, your lips — the way one eyebrow is up a bit higher than the other, the dimple in your chin — none of those things changed, and *that's* what I want! When you pull your head out of your ass and deal with your issues, come find me and *maybe* I'll still want you."

Jayden ran down the pier and I called after him, but he didn't stop. I picked up the fan magazine and stared at the cover photo. It was Skull Blasters and to the right was a page number with our interviews. I flipped to mine quickly and found my middle school and high school pictures. I re-read my interview and smiled. It was one of the first ones we ever did for a popular magazine. I was gushing about my mom and her cooking and how my grandfather and I always went rock hunting before he got sick. I stared at my picture. That was the guy Jayden wanted?

I leaned against the railing and stared out at the Pacific Ocean. A slight breeze blew in the smell of brine, and lights twinkled in the distance. If I wanted Jayden, I was going to have to put my ghosts to rest.

I truly believed I'd found my missing piece of the puzzle and the sound I needed.

Chapter 12

Jinx

I went home to Flagstaff the next day. I couldn't find Jayden anywhere and Evander refused to disclose his whereabouts. I decided not to pursue him until I could be what he wanted.

Me. The *real* me.

I was going to talk to my father, but I needed some down time before I went at him with both guns. I didn't care how much he's changed now. Back then, he'd made me feel like a freak. I *loved* boy bands back in middle school. I *did* have a crush on Lance Bass. I wanted to look like him, sound like him, and have everything he had. I had posters of The Backstreet Boys, NSYNC, and a few others on my wall, and I even practiced dance steps. I found guys attractive when I was thirteen, I got boners in school watching the athletes. My father found me jacking off to a poster and that was it. He took all my posters and CDs and told me if I kept listening to that kind of music, I'd end up gay and he was *not* going to have a gay son.

I crossed my living room to my CD player and opened the cabinet to my secret CD collection. I turned the volume up as high as it would go and stood in my backyard as *Bye, Bye, Bye* by NSYNC blasted out across the desert. I was startled to hear singing along my back wall and then Harley poked his head up over it. I laughed as Harley shouted the lyrics. We both began singing and I let Harley in the back gate. We danced around the pool, singing the lyrics at the top of our lungs. We went back in the house and I shut off the CD player, collapsing with laughter. Harley sprawled out on the couch holding his stomach.

"Dude! I didn't know you liked that music!" I laughed.

"I would say I don't, but then I wouldn't be able to explain knowing the lyrics."

"I thought you hated boy bands?"

"That was *you.* I never said such a thing."

I sat on the floor and regarded my best friend. He was laughing, but there was sadness behind those eyes.

"You saw your parents?"

"Yep."

"How did that go?"

"Same ol', same ol'. I gave them tickets for the finale."

"Harley." I shook my head. "I'm sorry."

"Well, that's why I'm here. Can I stay? I didn't want to be alone."

"I'm sure you're not alone. Where's Achilles?"

"I lost him somewhere on the freeway." Harley grinned.

"Are you sure about that?"

Harley's grin faded and I laughed.

"I need to find Jayden, but they won't tell me where he is." I sighed, rubbing my face.

"Well, we could play detective."

"I've got a better idea." I stood up and tilted my head to the side. "Achilles?"

"What?"

I jumped in the air as Achilles poked his head in through the back door.

"Nice try, Harley," Achilles said as he walked into my house. "Nice concert out back," he added.

"Blowing off some steam," I explained somewhat defensively. "I need your help."

Achilles dropped on the couch next to Harley, bouncing him into the air, and gave him a fierce look. He turned back to me and nodded his head. "What do you need?"

"Um, you're like Special Forces and stuff, right?"

"Former, but yes."

"Could you find someone for me?"

"Jayden?" Achilles searched my face.

"Yes."

"Should be able to give you a location in no time. In the meantime," Achilles glared at Harley. "If *you're* staying here, so am I."

"Is there some reason why you can't get off my ass?" Harley groused.

"Hang on, I've been waiting for this. I've got a list." Achilles reached into his pocket, pulled out his wallet and lifted out a piece of paper covered in barely legible scrawls. "Because you're unreasonable, rash, impulsive, impetuous, reckless, irrational, indiscreet, infantile, and flaky." He turned the paper and squinted. "And you're a chipmunk. Huh? Oops, sorry. That says 'childlike'."

"Thank you!" Harley batted his lashes.

"Where are the other Marvel Men?" I asked, smothering a laugh.

"Axel is with Gareth and Ransom, Buster and Hammer are with Rebel. I think they're playing pool in town."

"So, do you think Hammer and Buster might ever break into song?" Harley mused.

"No."

"Will you?"

"No."

I laughed as Harley gave Achilles his best pout. Many women had fallen prey to Harley Payne's pout.

We sat around watching Netflix for a while before I said goodnight. Harley was out, a slight snore his only contribution to the conversation. I needed to be up early to confront my father and find Jayden. I looked over my shoulder as I left the living room. Achilles was placing one of my throw blankets over a sleeping Harley. Harley needed someone to take care of him and Achilles fit that bill. I smiled as I watched them. I wanted that — someone who I could take care of and who could take care of me.

I needed Jayden.

~*~

I went to my parents' house in the morning. I needed to get my boxes from the attic and talk to Dad. No one was home when I got there, so I used my key to get in. The house was warm and smelled like coffee. I grabbed a cup on the way up to the attic. I stood at the bottom of the stairs and willed myself to go up there. Fucking thing freaked me out, like 'The Grudge' was up there or something. I shivered and took a deep breath. I pulled the string and stairs folded out.

I climbed halfway up and reached up to hit the light switch, illuminating the attic. The smell of mothballs assaulted me and I swiped at a cobweb. A row of boxes lined one wall and I headed that way. My name was on a few of them and I pulled one down, searching through the contents. The first one contained some old books and pictures. I dragged another one down and found some of my old baseball hats and clothes.

The third box held a lot of the things my grandfather had left to me, including his old military uniform and some pictures of him behind his drum set. I traced his face with my finger. I missed him. I missed having coffee with him and laughing about bullshit stuff. I caught sight of another box across from me and dragged it over. I opened it and gasped. It was all my posters and CDs that my father took from me. Why keep them? Why not just throw them out like he said he would? The front door shut downstairs and paper rustled. I poked my head out of the attic.

"Hello?"

"Josiah?" my father called out.

"Yes, I'm up in the attic."

"I'll come up."

"No, I really want to come out. Can you help me with the boxes?"

"Sure."

I waited for my father to appear at the bottom of the ladder before I slid the first box at him. It was the one with my posters and CDs.

"Why didn't you destroy them like you said you would?" I yelled.

"Because I couldn't," he said quietly.

I lowered another box to him, which he caught, and then another and another. Finally, I didn't have any more of mine to move.

"Josiah, please come down so that I can talk to you."

I grabbed my now-cold coffee and descended the steps, moving by him on my way to the kitchen. He followed behind me silently. I poured another cup of coffee and dropped into one of the kitchen chairs. He poured his own cup and then stood there, staring into his cup as if it would tell him what to say.

"Well?" I glared at him.

"I'm not perfect, Josiah; none of us are. I've made mistakes with you that I'm ashamed of. I thought it was a failure on my part that you were attracted to boys, that I didn't spend enough time with you."

"No, I spent time with Grandpa, he must have made me gay," I said wryly.

"I know that's not what happened. My father never had a problem with gays, he was in the military and surrounded by people from all walks of life. He didn't teach me bigotry, I did that on my own. My friends in school, we always knew when a boy liked his bread buttered on a different side."

"Well, that's … a different expression."

"We thought they were weaker, more feminine than us. And I'm ashamed to say, I was a bully." My father shook his head sadly.

"I like women *and* men, Pop. I just couldn't get either when I was younger."

"You're that same Josiah, son. You have a very caring heart and the mind of a poet. You see things no one else does. You see beauty all around where we see nothing. I was very wrong to treat you as I did and I am so truly sorry." My father wiped at his eyes.

I had only seen my dad cry twice   when my grandfather got sick, and at his funeral. Well, that took the wind out of my sails and my anger vanished. I stood up and crossed to my father.

"I know you love me, I knew it back then, too. I just … I wanted to be me."

"And I love *you*. I know I should have become the man I am now back then, and it took cancer to make me see that life is short. You were with me every step of the way, staying home with me, cleaning up after me when your mom had to work. After everything I said and did to you, you still took care of me."

"You're my Pops." I smiled.

"I am so very proud of you, Josiah."

"Yeah? Even if I'm falling for a guy?"

My father's eyes widened. "You're falling in love?"

"Yes, did you hear the part where it's a guy?"

"That's of no consequence. My son is finally falling in love? I want to hear all about this man."

"Are you on meds?" I stared at him.

"Come! Sit! Let us talk about this man."

I told my dad all about Jayden. He listened attentively and even made some suggestions on how to get Jayden back. All in all, it was one weird morning. I made blueberry muffins, and when Mom came home, we all sat down together like we used to.

As a family.

To say Mom was excited about my potential love life was an understatement. I showed them pictures of Jayden that I looked up online and my mother patted her chest.

"He is so beautiful, Josiah! You've done well." She waggled her brows.

"He likes me for me, ya know? The guy I used to be before I became Jinx- asshole-Jett."

"No swear words at the table," my mother giggled.

"You were not an ass, Josiah, you were angry," Dad pointed out.

"That's no excuse for the way I treated some of those women. In my next interview, I'll apologize to them."

"Are you staying for dinner?" Mom asked hopefully.

"Yes. Are you making mac and cheese?"

"But of course!"

My phone beeped with a text from Achilles. He'd found Jayden and was tracking him.

"Can I get that mac and cheese to go?"

"Of course. What is it?" my mother asked.

"They've located Jayden."

"Why are you still here?" my father smiled.

"I'll just make you a to-go package." My mother hurried off to the kitchen.

"Jinx?"

"Yes?"

"Good luck."

"Thanks, Pop."

Chapter 13

Jayden

I took a deep breath and concentrated on the road in front of me. After going back to Phoenix for one night, I'd finally gotten around to unpacking my boxes from home. Quite a few things were missing. Namely, the penguin collection from my grandmother. I called Sebastian immediately and he put me on a jet to Columbus, Georgia, which had the nearest airport to my hometown. My parents wanted to see me? Well, they were going to get me. It was no fluke or accident that the crystal penguins weren't in my boxes; that was done deliberately, just like them hiding my drum set.

It was weird to be back in Alabama after being gone for a year. I crossed the bridge and headed into Phenix City. Nothing much had changed since the last time I was here.

My parents wanted me to go to the University of Alabama, but I wanted out of Alabama, so I went to the University of Georgia instead. Not that I was opposed to the Crimson Tide, I cheered for them, in fact. But I wanted a change of scenery.

My mind wandered back to Jinx on the pier. Did he really think I wanted him just for the way he looked? That hurt more than anything. The worst part about all of this was that I was falling in love with the asshole. Yeah, he was a jerk sometimes, but after hearing why he felt the way he did, I kind of understood him even more.

I pulled up to my parents' house and just sat in the car. It seemed so long ago that I was here at the yellow house with white shutters and a huge American flag on the front porch. I got out of the car, marched up the front steps, and banged on the front door. I could hear footsteps on the other side, and then the door swung open and my mom stood there with her expression going from annoyed to sheepish.

"Jayden?"

"Yeah, Jayden." I opened the screen door and walked past her. "Where's the penguin collection, Ma?"

"What? No hello?" She shut the door and turned to face me.

"Hello. Where's my collection?"

"Would you like some sweet tea?" My mother brushed past me and went to the kitchen.

"Ma! Where is it?"

"We haven't seen you in months and all you want to know about is where your grandmother's collection is?" She pinned me with a hard stare.

"It's *my* collection, and if I remember correctly, you and Dad kicked me out! Did you really expect regular visits?" I shouted.

"We were surprised! We didn't know how to deal with your news!"

"Well, I didn't stop being your son because I'm gay," I drawled. "But I'm certain that most experts recommend going with the knee-jerk, 'make them feel unloved, freakish, and outcast reaction'."

"We handled it badly, I admit that."

"Nooo. Ya think?" I placed my hands on my hips. "Where's the collection?"

"Do you even want to know how your father and I have been doing while you've been off gallivanting, making your millions? He lost his job and we've been struggling to pay the mortgage and bills! We housed you, clothed you—"

"Whoa! Hold up a second. I didn't ask to be born, so your taking care of me from birth to eighteen was *your* responsibility! After that, well, I thank you for putting me somewhat through college and housing me after the age of eighteen. Is that what it's all about? You want money from me? Well, hell, let me just write you a check then! I'll be out of your hair as soon as I have my drums and my crystal penguins."

"We sold the penguins," my mother said quietly.

"I'm sorry," I said slowly. "Could you repeat that?"

"We needed the money! You weren't here and—"

"Well, whose fault is it that I wasn't here, huh? Y'all kicked me out! Who did you sell them to? A collector?"

"No, your father took them to the pawn shop."

"*The pawn shop*?! Oh. My. God! Do you know how much those are worth? Those were *Swarovski* crystal! You could have gotten thousands for them and you took them to a pawn shop?" I dragged my hands down my face with a frustrated sigh. "Which one, Ma? I might be able to get them back."

"It's been months, Jayden. I doubt they're still there."

My whole world fell out from beneath me at those words. My grandmother's pride and joy, the one thing I'd held onto, was gone. Sold to someone who probably didn't even know what he or she had, and certainly didn't have any sentimental attachment to them. My eyes burned and my chest tightened.

"Which one?" I asked again.

"I don't know, the one off of U.S. 280, I think." My mother approached me. "Jayden ..."

"Are my drums still here?"

"Yes."

"Good. I'll be getting them right now."

I pushed past my mother and took the stairs to the basement. Thankfully, I'd rented a van when I landed at the airport and I could pack my drums into it. They all had a fitted carrying case, so I could ship them home. I packed them up, stopping occasionally to swipe at the tears cascading down my cheeks. How could they? The rest of my day would be spent trying to track down my penguins. My mother came down the stairs as I was loading my snare into its case.

"Jayden, I'm sorry. I really am."

"About which part? Kicking me out or selling my stuff?"

"You wouldn't talk to us! We had no choice!"

"*You* kicked *me* out!" I practically screamed. "Why should I talk to you? I am NOT the bad guy here, Mom!"

"We were wrong, all right? We didn't handle it the way we should have, but that is no reason to keep punishing us! We made a mistake!"

"Yeah, you made a lot of them. And maybe I'd take your 'apology' a little more seriously if it had come before I came back here and realized you're only saying it because you need money and are hoping I'll be your cash cow." I snapped the lock down and grabbed one of the heavier cases, lugging it up the stairs. My mother followed me out to the van. I hit the key fob and the back opened automatically. I shoved the case in and turned back to the house.

"Jayden, please listen."

"Where is dad?" I asked as I headed back towards the house.

"He's trying to find a job, Jayden. We're going to lose the house if we can't come up with the mortgage."

"I'll write you a check, and then I want you to stay out of my life. Do you understand? Just give me the name of the pawn shop."

I packed up my drum set while my mother followed me back and forth, babbling about how sorry she was and wringing her hands. Well, that was wonderful, wasn't it? I couldn't seem to care at the moment. Did that make me an asshole? Probably, but they couldn't lift a finger to answer my calls when I was practically starving in Los Angeles. Why should I believe there was even a grain of sincerity to her apology since neither she nor my father had made any effort to talk to me since throwing me out, much less apologize to me. This one seemed awfully convenient.

My mother stood off to the side of the van, wringing her hands. She looked older than I remembered. I pulled my backpack out of the passenger seat and took my checkbook from the front pocket. I wrote out a check, using the hood of the van as a table. I ripped it out and handed it to her without a word. She gave me the name of the pawn shop where she thought my father had taken the penguins. Without another word, I jumped in the van and closed the door, firing it up. I left without looking back.

~*~

The pawn shop my father took the penguins to refused to tell me who had bought them. The clerk said something about a warrant or something to get the names. What the hell? I checked into a hotel and sunk into the bed, frustrated. My grandmother loved me unconditionally, was always there for me when I was sad. I was with her when she took her last breath, and in those final days, we had so many great talks. She had asked me to bring in her collection and place the shiny penguins around her hospital room. During the day, the sun's rays would catch them just right, painting the room in a rainbow of colors. I wiped my eyes and rolled to my side. I felt so alone. I missed the guys; they'd become my family. I grabbed my phone and dialed Evander's phone. He picked up on the third ring.

"Tally ho!"

"Is that a gay bar?"

"No, that's Tally whacker."

I cracked up.

"How are you, Evander?"

"Missing my country boy. You sound sad. Did Jinx try to call you?"

"I saw him on the pier and you know that because you told him where I was."

"I couldn't help it. Did he hurt you further?"

"He thinks I want him for his face." Evander snorted on the other end and I chuckled.

"Did the boy not hear your interview? You said 'have you seen him' and then went on to talk about what he looks like when he plays. I think everyone thought you meant his actual looks. When are you coming back?"

"Tomorrow. I got my drums and shipped them off."

"Then why do you sound like someone ran over your favorite pet?"

"Because my parents sold my penguin collection, that's why."

"The one your grandmother gave you?"

"Yes. I wrote them a check and told them to stay out of my life."

"Did they at least apologize for their behavior?"

"Mom did, for what it was worth. Dad wasn't home."

"I'm so sorry, Jayden. I'll make sure I have blueberry muffins for you when you come back."

"That's so sweet." I grinned.

There was a knock on my hotel room door and I cocked a brow. Who the fuck knew where I was staying? I didn't tell my parents.

"Evander?"

"Yes?"

"Did you tell anyone where I am?"

"No. Why?"

"Someone just knocked on my door." The knock sounded again and I crossed the room to the door, peeking out the peephole. Jinx Jett stood on the other side of the door.

"Shit, it's Jinx," I whispered.

"Open the door! He followed you? He cares, Jayden. Let the idiot in."

"Gotta go!"

"Get laid!" Evander laughed.

I hung up and opened the door. Jinx stood there with his hands stuffed in the pockets of his faded jeans. His head tilted and he searched my face.

"What's wrong?" he asked.

I backed up and let him in. I shut the door and then leaned against it.

"What are you doing here, Jinx?"

"I wanted to see you ... to explain."

"You already did that at the pier, Jinx."

Jinx took my hand and palmed my cheek with his other one. "What's wrong? You've been crying."

So I told him. I broke down and cried because I couldn't hold it in anymore. Jinx held me, rocked me, and soothed me. I wrapped my arms around him and held on as the flood of emotions hit me like a tsunami. Warm lips grazed my temple and Jinx's hand fell to the base of my spine. I needed him. I wanted him. And, God help me, I always would. I knew that now. I lifted my head and kissed his chin, running my hands down his back and to his butt, gripping his ass cheeks and squeezing.

"Jayden," Jinx gasped. "This isn't a good idea; you're vulnerable."

"Want you," I rasped. "Need you."

"Then take me," Jinx agreed quietly.

I pulled slightly away from him. Our eyes met and I realized what he meant. My hands trembled and my knees shook as the reality of the situation crashed down on me. Could I really take Jinx Jett? The guy had never been with a man in that way. I searched his eyes and he nodded, completely committed to what he'd said. Our lips met and Jinx walked me to the bed, removing my shirt along the way. His hands slid up my back and gripped the tops of my shoulders, pulling me closer to him. I fumbled to get his shirt off as we tumbled onto the bed, a mass of tangled limbs and searching lips.

Jinx managed to get his pants and boxers off and I hovered above him, drinking in the sight of his sinewy muscles and fabulous skin. I leaned down and pressed a kiss to his chest, licking across one pebbled nipple. Jinx's back arched and his dick flexed on his abdomen. I treated his other nipple to a lick and nibble before I slid down his chest, licking his treasure trail and making slow circles with my tongue around his belly button. My hand cupped his nuts, massaging them and rolling them in my palm. Jinx stilled my hand and I glanced up.

"Lube and condom?" he asked.

I leaned over the side of the bed and grabbed my backpack. I had a special pocket where I stored emergency staples. I pulled out the tube of lube and a condom, placing them by the pillows. Jinx pulled me back down and proceeded to give me the slowest, most passionate kiss I'd ever gotten. I was lost. My head was spinning, my body tingling with every touch Jinx made. I wanted to feel every inch of him, *taste* every inch of him.

We broke from the kiss, Jinx's breathing slightly labored. I placed my hand on his inner thigh and smoothed it down, my palm passing over fine, soft hair. I leaned in to kiss him again as I rubbed his perineum, soft strokes of my finger passing over his hole with every other swipe. Jinx shivered under me and I lifted my head and grabbed the lube. Our eyes locked as I lubricated two of my fingers. Jinx nodded and I rubbed his hole slowly.

"Jayden." Jinx took my face in his hands.

"Shhh." I kissed him again before sliding a finger inside him.

Jinx's eyes went wide as I stretched him, searching for the knot of nerves that would make him lose his mind. He gasped and softly cursed, and I smiled. I had found it. I rubbed it relentlessly, watching Jinx fly apart beneath me. His moans and whimpers filled the room around me. God, he was beautiful in the throes of passion. I added another finger, pushing Jinx to his limits. His dick was hard, bouncing on his abs as he writhed on the bed, squirming on my fingers. I removed them slowly; Jinx's eyes opened and he stared at me. He raised a hand and touched my cheek. He looked so small just then, like someone lost who needed his hand held. I sheathed my dick and positioned myself against his opening. His eyes closed and I leaned in, kissing his lips softly.

"Look at me," I whispered.

Storm-gray eyes opened and focused on mine. I pushed in just a bit and Jinx's mouth formed a silent O. Inch by excruciating inch, I sunk my dick into Jinx's ass, trying to hold back what I knew was going to rock me to my core. I'd had sex before, but never with someone I cared about. Molten heat surrounded my dick, gripping and expanding as I pushed further inside. I gripped Jinx's deflating cock and began to pump him slowly as I pulled back a little. When I got some response, I pushed back in, making sure I did it slowly, and Jinx's ass welcomed me. I stopped when my balls touched his hot skin. Jinx was breathing hard, trying to maintain our eye contact.

"Tell me what it feels like," I whispered as I pulled back out just as slowly.

"Hot, full, burning ..." Jinx panted.

I thrust back in and he gasped; his fingers gripped my biceps and his head fell back, eyes closed.

"Hey now, keep your eyes on me."

He lifted his head and opened his eyes. I kept him with me as I pumped in and out, in and out, our bodies slapping, sweat dripping and mouths meeting. God, I'd never felt like this with anyone! Jinx and I fit, we meshed in every damn way and I realized then that I wanted him for always. He held my face and kissed me as I continued to drive into him, faster and faster, building up his need and mine. I rubbed his prostate over and over, keeping my thrusts at an angle and attacking his mouth as I jacked him off. His dick flexed in my palm and fire was building in my gut. Desperate to come, I jacked him off faster, keeping it in time with my forceful thrusts.

"Oh ... oh shit!" Jinx shouted.

Ropes of cum arced from his dick and my own orgasm hit, almost knocking me unconscious. I fell over Jinx and wrapped my arms around him. Lips grazed my ear and then soft kisses rained on my neck. I lifted my head and met his lips. Our tongues glided together and I moaned in his mouth. God, I loved the way this man tasted. I broke the kiss and pulled out of his body slowly, making sure to hold the base of the condom. I threw it into the trash bin by the bed and went to the bathroom.

When I came back to the bed, Jinx was on his back, one hand behind his head and the other on his abs. I wiped up the mess on his stomach and chest and then bent down to kiss his belly button.

"You okay?" I asked.

"I didn't know it could feel so good," he admitted.

"Oh, I haven't even done half the shit I know how to do." I waggled my brows.

"There's more?" Jinx's eyes widened in surprise.

"Yeah, there's more," I said huskily as I draped over him and kissed him.

Jinx wrapped his arms around me and flipped me to my back, deepening the kiss. It felt so right in his arms, as though this was where I belonged forever. Jinx kissed my eyes, then my nose, and came back to my lips, rubbing them lightly with his own.

"I like this," he said. "You fit perfectly. It is always like this?"

"Like what?"

"You know, like ... you're trying to find that perfect sound, the one that makes you vibrate and your heart pound like a bass drum, that symphony in your head and the tickling of notes across your skin that lets you know you've found the one." Jinx blinked. "Does that make sense?"

It did and that was what scared the ever-loving shit out of me. I'd found my sound in Jinx, the one that made me sing from the inside out.

"Yeah, it does," I whispered.

"I don't want to move." Jinx yawned.

"Don't then. Stay right here." I snuggled into his chest and closed my eyes.

"Jayden?"

"Yeah?"

"We'll get your penguins back."

"You don't think it's stupid?"

Jinx looked down at me and kissed my nose. "You're talking to the guy with the rock collection from his grandfather."

"Yeah, but that's cool."

"Penguins are awesome. Did you know that male penguins will search the beach for that   "

"Perfect rock?" I smiled. "Yeah, I know. Surprised you know that."

"My dad and I watched a lot of National Geographic when he was sick."

"On the pier, you said there was more about your relationship with your father."

"Yes, I had it out with him. When I was younger, he caught me jacking off to a boy band poster   "

I snorted.

"Yeah, yeah, I know. He ripped them all down and took my CDs, telling me if I kept listening to that, I'd turn gay."

"What is it with parents and the notion that we *turn* gay?"

"Gareth said he's always known I was bi. I've kept that part of me hidden for so long, I don't know how to process all this."

"Just take it one day at a time. So, you also said you ate a lot of blueberry muffins."

"I did, I still do, although someone keeps eating them all at the hotel."

"That would be me." I lazily raised a hand. "Sorry, they're my favorite."

Jinx chuckled and nuzzled my cheek with his nose. "What a pair we are, huh?"

I looked into Jinx's eyes. It was like looking up at the sky on a cloudy day. He was just perfect, *now and then*. I couldn't believe I was in bed with him and I'd just made love to him. Oh God. I was in love with Jinx Jett.

"You okay?" Jinx's brows furrowed as he watched my face.

"Yeah. Just tired."

"Can I stay...you know, here...with you?"

I kissed him then, trying to convey how I felt. I didn't want to be Jinx's play toy, the secret he kept behind closed doors. And I didn't know if he was ready to be out with me just yet. I didn't know if I was willing to stay a secret. As much as I loved him, I didn't know how he felt about me.

I couldn't risk my heart.

"Sure," I whispered across his lips.

I watched him sleep for hours. I couldn't help it. He looked so peaceful when he slept. I traced his bottom lip with my finger and smiled when his nose twitched. He might have let me make love to him, but what did he want from me? How could we work anyway? We would both tour, spend months apart from each other. I sighed and kissed him softly.

"We'll always have tonight, Jinx. I'll never forget it."

Chapter 14

Jayden

Jinx was still asleep when I woke up. I touched his face and kissed him. He whimpered a little and turned to his side. I felt like shit for what I was about to do, but I knew I was right. Jinx might think he wanted something with me, but by the light of day, he would know he couldn't truly be out with me. Not a heavy metal rocker and a boy band singer. I found the hotel pad of paper and scribbled out a note for him. I wasn't going to leave him this time without some form of explanation.

I dressed quickly and grabbed my backpack. I took one last look at the man I'd fallen for before quietly slipping out.

I took the van back to the airport and boarded Sebastian's private jet. I needed to get back to L.A. for the finale and I still had work to do with the guys. I reclined my seat back and closed my eyes. God forgive me for leaving Jinx the way I had. I'd always want him; that would never change.

Evander was waiting for me at LAX and we jumped into the limo that would take us back to the hotel. I looked out the window as we hit the freeway. God, I missed Jinx already. I knew he had been awake for hours and was probably pissed I left him. I looked down at my phone, but I didn't have any missed calls or texts. My stomach plummeted. Evander's hand crept into mine and I squeezed it, glancing over at him.

"You love him," Evander observed quietly.

"Yeah. I do."

"Tell me what happened."

I explained everything on the ride back to the hotel my parents, Jinx, and the night we spent together. Evander listened and didn't interrupt. Just hearing myself say the words made me want to slap myself for leaving him. He'd given me a piece of himself and I'd walked right out of his life.

"You're scared, Jayden, and it's normal." Evander leaned into me. "Don't walk away from Jinx; I truly believe he cares for you."

"He hasn't said he loves me."

"He gave himself to you, isn't that enough?"

"I don't know anymore! You know how he is! A different girl every night. How stupid am I to think that I'm better than all of them and he'll settle down with me? I'm not that naïve!"

"That man took the time to track you down and then he opened himself up to you. I don't see Jinx Jett doing that for anyone but you."

"I don't know what to do. I'm fucking terrified, Evander."

"I want to belt you in the forehead with a scone."

"Well, that's harsh." I stared at my phone, willing it to ring.

"Call him, tell him you're sorry for leaving him."

"I will, just not right now."

"Chicken shit."

"Shut up."

~*~

I still hadn't heard from Jinx, and now I was really scared. What had I done? I had to pull myself together because I had a performance to do. The guys and I practiced our routine with the choreographer again, who decided I was her whipping boy that day. I couldn't concentrate for shit. The twins were covered in sweat, as was Evander by the time she let us go for the day. I fell to the floor and stared up at the ceiling with my arms outstretched to the sides.

"Lord, please make it swift."

Evander fell next to me, panting and cursing. "That woman is crazy. There isn't an ounce of fat on her."

Sebastian walked into the room and surveyed all of us sweating, cursing, and breathing hard. His lips lifted in a smile and he squatted down, crossing his arms.

"Are we ready for the double elimination tonight?" he asked.

"As long as Scott gets voted off," I said.

"I know who's staying and who's' going." Sebastian waggled his brows.

"Hint?" I tilted my head.

"Nope. Get showered and get to the studio."

Sebastian left and I pulled myself up. Hopefully I would see Jinx tonight. Maybe I could talk to him, explain why I left the way I did. Although, my note pretty much said it all.

The guys and I showered and dressed, then headed to the studio. There was a line outside the door and all the way around the building as we entered the main door. We stopped and took pictures with fans and smiled for the cameras. We all waved and headed inside. Seats were filling as we took ours in the front row. More screams erupted as we turned to face the crowd behind us. Jericho and Zeke were standing near the stage and I crossed over to them, hugging them both.

"You guys are going to do just fine. I just know you'll both make the cut." I assured them.

"Thanks, Jayden," Zeke said sincerely.

I spotted Gareth walking in with his husband and I waved, hoping to get his attention. Gareth grinned and dragged Axel over to me.

"Hey!" I said, hugging him. "Have you see Jinx?"

"He called and said he had some things to do but would be back for the finale." Gareth took my hands. "Did something happen?"

"Can we talk after this?" I asked.

"Yeah, dinner?"

"Sure."

I sat nervously through four acts, biting my nails as I waited to see who was getting kicked off. I crossed my fingers that both Jericho and Zeke would stay. Both of them deserved to be up there. Sebastian took the stage after Jericho finished and called all four contestants up. I was on the edge of my seat as Sebastian took the slip of paper out of his pocket.

"The first contestant going home tonight is ..."

"Please let it be Scott," I whispered. Gareth chuckled next to me and I laughed.

"Scott. I'm so sorry, Scott." Sebastian shook Scott's hand and then Scott took the stairs down. He passed by us and we all grinned.

The music started again, that foreboding music all reality shows love to use whether kicking someone off or letting them stay.

"Staying tonight is ..."

I held my breath.

"Jericho!"

The guys and I jumped up, clapping so hard I knew our hands would be red.

One of the female contestants was next to go and that meant Zeke was staying. The auditorium was filled with cheers and clapping as Zeke and Jericho took a bow. I was giddy that my two favorite guys were staying. The sad part was only one of them would win. I hoped Sebastian would put them together. I thought they sounded awesome.

I leaned into Evander's ear and let him know I was going out with Gareth. He squeezed my hand and smiled. I followed Gareth and his huge husband out the side doors and into the lobby; paparazzi and fans surrounded us immediately. Gareth shot his husband a look and smiled for the cameras, his arms wrapped around adoring male and female fans alike.

"He's pretty stubborn, huh?" I asked Axel.

"You have no idea." Axel sighed.

Gareth finally disengaged himself and we piled into a limo. I sat across from Gareth and Axel. They seem so … different? I guess that worked for them, though. Axel was well over six foot and Gareth was much, much shorter and their body size difference was ridiculous.

"So, tell me." Gareth sat forward, clasping his hands together.

So I did. I told Gareth everything about my trip to Alabama, how Jinx found me, and the night we shared. I didn't go into *too* much detail about the sex, just that we had it. Gareth smiled when I was finished.

"I knew he had feelings for you."

"Well, I may have just fucked it all up."

"I don't think so. When Harley spoke to Jinx on the phone, he didn't seem upset, just preoccupied, and then he called Axel and the guys." Gareth turned to his husband. "Anything you care to share?"

"Nope." Axel shook his head. "I'm sworn to secrecy."

I pouted.

"That may work on Jinx, but it doesn't work on me." Axel lifted a brow.

"Meanie," I joked.

"So, what do you want for dinner? I'm in the mood for a bloody steak."

"Bloody steak it is," I laughed.

Sitting with Gareth Wolf and his husband was a little surreal. Never in my life did I think I'd be this close to someone so famous. The first time I met Gareth in the mall, though, I could see the kind of person he was: kind, sweet, and caring. He treated me like someone special *before* I was someone special.

"I gotta say, that day in the mall? Jinx couldn't stop admiring your ass." Gareth nearly fell over laughing.

"Really?" my eyes widened.

"Oh yeah," Axel agreed.

"He admitted you were all that to me. I always knew deep down that Jinx liked both sexes, he just buried it deep to try to please his father."

"Well, he told me he had it out with his dad, so I guess that's water under the bridge."

"I'm glad." Gareth leaned forward and took my hands. "Don't give up on him. I know he cares for you."

I swallowed hard. I'd been the one to cast him aside. I just hope he forgave me when I came crawling back to him. I smiled at Gareth.

"I won't."

Chapter 15

Jinx

I held Jayden's note in my hand and read it for the thousandth time.

Jinx,

I know you're going to think I'm an asshole, but I can't do this. I know you think you want me   all of me but when it comes down to it, I don't think you're ready to be out and I'm not going to force you to do it for me. I've never felt for anyone what I feel for you, which is why I'm willing to give you up. You say you care for me, but words are just that. Words. I hope you find someone you can be yourself with and please know that I'll always cherish the time we spent together.

Love, Jayden.

At least he left me a note this time, but for him to think I was going to let him bed me and then walk away? I shook my head. Hell no. No one takes my ass and gets to walk out of my life. He was mine and I was going to prove it to him. Which is why I needed to pull myself out of this funk and let the guys in on my plan. I'd spent the last twenty-four hours running all over Alabama. I just hoped I hadn't screwed things up too much.

We were still waiting for Rebel to arrive. Seems he'd had a late night of his own. Gareth was sitting on Axel's lap, looking like he'd just rolled out of bed after a good fuck. Harley was half asleep on the chair in the corner and Achilles was standing with his back to us, looking out the window. Hammer, Buster, and Stan were sitting on the couch waiting for me to tell them my plan. I had no idea if they'd help me.

Well, I knew Gareth would.

The door to the suite opened and Rebel walked in, wet. From a shower I presumed, but with Rebel, you never really knew.

"Rebel." I nodded.

"The word of the day is bukkake." Rebel sat on the couch between Stan and Hammer. "Please use it in a sentence."

Harley opened his mouth and Achilles pointed a finger at him.

"No."

"But   "

"No." Achilles said, more firmly this time.

"But it was good one!" Harley protested.

"Do I even want to know what bukkake is?" Stan cocked a brow.

"No," we all answered in unison.

"So." Rebel spread his arms out along the back of the couch and crossed his legs. "What do you want from us?"

"Okay, you guys have to know by now how I feel about Jayden."

"Oh yeah." Everyone nodded and babbled at once.

"So I need him to know I'm not kidding around this time. I have real feelings for the guy."

"Okay, well I thought you told him that?" Harley's brows furrowed.

"Yes, but actions speak louder than words. I'm willing to do whatever it takes to make him see how much I care about him."

Rebel sat forward and searched my face. "Dude, you fell in love with him."

"Yeah, I did," I admitted. My face flushed and I averted my eyes.

"Aw, Jinx!" Gareth wiped his eyes. "I'm so happy for you!"

"Thanks, but this is where the hard part comes in. I have an idea, but I need you guys to back me up."

"You know we will," Harley insisted.

"You may not after I tell you my plan."

"Whatever, dude. You know we will." Rebel winked.

"I also want to thank *you* guys," I jerked my chin toward Axel, Buster, Hammer, and Achilles, "as well as your boss, Mac, for your help with my scavenger hunt."

Hammer grunted and I grinned. "Well, that's a good sign."

Achilles chuckled from his post by the window.

"So, I suggest we get our asses over to the studio so I can fill you in and we can practice."

"Practice what? We already know our songs," Harley chuckled.

"You'll see."

~*~

I stood in the center of the stage with the guys and told them what I needed. I thought Rebel was going to pass out. I knew it was a lot to ask, but I also knew these guys would bleed for me. I'd called my parents earlier and messengered over the tickets for the finale. My mother couldn't stop crying and kept saying how happy she was for me. I just hoped everything I was going to do was enough. I knew my reputation preceded me, but I also knew that once I'd set my mind, I was all in.

And I was all in with Jayden.

The guys and I practiced for most of the afternoon. The only thing I needed was a drummer. I headed back to the hotel and looked for Jayden's guys. I had to get into his room before the finale. I searched the dining room, then the pool. I'd almost given up when I ran into the twins coming down the hall.

"Um." I looked from one to the other. I had no idea which was which.

"That's Dimas." One of them pointed to the other. "I'm Dimos."

"Do either of you play drums?" I asked hopefully.

"I do." Dimos nodded. "Why?"

"I need a favor. Well, actually, I need two of them."

"Okayyy." Dimas said slowly. "Just know we'd never betray Jayden."

"What I have in mind is far from betrayal. Can you let me in his room? I promise you'll be okay with it."

Dimos cocked his head to the side, assessing me. I smiled and hooked my arm through his.

"Come with me to my room, I'll show you what I have for Jayden."

"Is this a come on?" Dimas asked. "Because I want in that sandwich."

"Sorry, my heart belongs to one man only." I winked.

"Good answer," Dimas chuckled.

I started walking down the hall, then stopped suddenly. "Wait a minute, are you *all* gay?"

"Evander's on the fence, but my brother and me? Oh yeah," Dimos laughed.

~*~

The night of the finale, I was shaking with excitement. I'd put my plan into action. I'd avoided Jayden so that when the plan went into effect, he'd truly be surprised. I twirled my drumstick between my fingers as I searched the crowd. I found my parents in the front row and descended the stairs to greet them. Mom hugged me, grabbed my face, and planted a kiss on both cheeks.

"I am so proud of you!" she gushed.

"I have to hand it to you, Josiah, you are very romantic." My father patted my shoulder.

"I just hope this goes over well," I said, searching for Jayden.

The lights lowered and the theme song for the show started playing. I kissed my mom and hugged my dad, taking the steps two at a time back up to the stage.

"Good evening ladies and gentlemen and welcome to the finale of Singers! Tonight's show promises to bring you excitement and drama!" Sebastian laughed. "Now, sit back and enjoy last season's winners, the London Boys!"

I hid behind the curtain as it opened to reveal Jayden and his band lined up with their heads down. They all wore faded, holey jeans with white T-shirts and Converse sneakers. The music started and their video was playing on a huge flat screen above them, showing all of the guys playing instruments. My original thought that all boy bands just sang na-na-na-naaa was officially blown out the window. Evander belted out the lyrics as the guys danced their choreographed steps around him and then I froze. Jayden opened his mouth and began singing. I stood there with my mouth dropped open as Jayden stood at the front of the stage, his voice wrapping me in its warmth. The crowd was going crazy as they all took their turn singing the lyrics. Jayden's hips swiveled and then he and the guys fell back on one hand, pumping the air with their hips. Girls screamed, and I kinda think I might have, too. The lyrics reminded me of our story. They repeated the chorus, all of them sliding one at a time across the stage on their knees. To finish, they all held up a hand and their heads fell forward. The crowd stood up, screaming, clapping, and whistling.

"Jinx!" Gareth grabbed my arm. "Come on!"

I followed Gareth to the other side of the stage where Sebastian was waiting for us. At first, he hadn't been on board with what I wanted to do, until I suggested to him that the ratings would go through the roof and it would get tons of airplay on the entertainment shows. Then he couldn't wait to help. Sebastian threw me a grin and then took me by the bicep.

"If you hurt that boy in any way, I'll cut off your testicles."

Somehow, the British accent made it sound less threatening. I shook my head clear. "I won't. Sebastian, why would I be doing this unless I was all in?"

"You're a good kid, Jinx. Good luck out there."

My heart hammered and I took a deep breath. This was it. My grand plan to make Jayden see how serious I was. Rebel and Harley put their arms around me and hugged me. I closed my eyes. I was so very lucky to have these guys in my life. They were willing to do anything for me, for love.

"If I lose cool points because of this, I'm blaming you, Jinx," Rebel threatened jokingly.

"Hands in!" Stan called out.

The six of us stood in a circle and put our hands in.

"Let's do this!" Harley shouted.

"Hell yeah!"

Chapter 16

Jayden

I was so excited, I almost peed myself! We were minutes from learning who had won the competition and I was crossing my fingers for both Jericho and Zeke. I was so happy Zeke had gotten this far. I had already done my number and was now back in the seating area. I felt a poke in my back and turned to see my parents behind me.

"How…?" I stammered.

"Your boyfriend stopped by the house. Grilled your father and me. He gave us tickets to the show."

"I want you to have this back, son." My father pressed the check I'd written into my hand. "We just want you in our lives. Keep the check if that proves we mean it. You've got a good man there."

Jinx had stopped by my parents' house? Why hadn't he said anything to me? Then again, he'd been avoiding me for two days. I stared at my parents and an ache formed in my chest. I pressed the check back into my father's hand. "Pay off the house, okay? We'll talk more after the show."

I was so focused on my parents that I didn't even notice Sebastian hit the stage or the cameraman counting down to live.

"Ladies and gentleman! We have a special performance for you tonight! I think you'll enjoy this, so please sit back and enjoy the Skull Blasters!"

I whirled around to the stage and my eyes widened as the curtain pulled back and a spotlight illuminated a grand piano. Jinx walked onstage and the crowd went crazy.

"Good evening, everyone. I know this isn't our normal music, but there's a guy out there who needs to know how I feel."

There was a collective gasp throughout the audience, but Jinx just smiled. He walked to the piano and sat down. He positioned the mic toward his mouth and then leaned in.

"Here's my action, Jayden. This is for you."

My mouth fell open and then musical notes filled the air. Jinx began playing the piano and I moved closer to the stage.

"Isn't that …?" Evander began, next to me.

"The Backstreet Boys' *Incomplete*," I answered in awe. "I didn't even know he could play the piano."

"I didn't even know you knew that song," Evander chuckled.

"Shh!" I smacked his chest with the back of my hand.

The stage lights came up and the rest of the band was behind Jinx playing along. I stared as I recognized Dimos behind my drum set. No wonder I couldn't find him after our set.

Jinx was in the moment. His eyes were closed, his fingers were moving fluidly over the keys. He was so beautiful, it actually took my breath away. His voice was absolute perfection and the words hit me like a freight train. My heart hurt for him, for the pain I must have caused him and yet, he still wanted me. I moved closer to the stage, as close as I could get without actually getting on it. I needed Jinx to see me, to know that I was there and how much I loved his gesture.

Finally, our eyes met and he locked on me, singing right to me. I held my hand up to my chest and he motioned me onstage. I shook my head and he winked, jerking his chin. The crowd went crazy yelling at me to get up there. Evander pushed me in the butt and I climbed the steps slowly. Jinx removed the mic from its stand and moved toward me. He pulled me into his arms and held the mic between us, urging me to sing with him. He palmed my cheek as we finished the song together. The crowd roared, jumped out of their seats and gave us a standing ovation. Jinx leaned in and kissed me, stealing my breath from me. The roar in the studio was so loud I was sure I was going to be deaf by morning. Jinx and I bowed together and then the curtain shut.

"Oh my God, Jinx!" I sobbed.

"Believe me now? You ever leave me like that again, and I'll have the guys hunt you down."

"Yeah right," I snorted, sniffling.

Jinx inclined his head toward the three behemoths standing offstage. They all nodded and I swallowed hard. "Hi guys." I half-waved.

Hammer grunted.

I turned back to Jinx. "I can't believe you did that!"

"I needed you to know that this isn't just a one-time thing with you. I'm not playing around, Jayden. You're it for me."

"God, how could I ever top that?"

"You could top me." Jinx winked, pulling me into his chest. "Again."

Sebastian poked his head through the curtain. "Hey guys, we need the stage. You know, for the finale and winner?" Sebastian grinned broadly.

"Yeah, okay. Thanks for letting me do that, Sebastian." Jinx put his hand out and Sebastian shook it.

"Are you kidding? The ratings are going through the roof! I think we busted social media pages. You two come back anytime and sing together. You sound fabulous."

"I think we'll stick to our own bands; maybe private singing only." Jinx smiled at me.

"Come on," I said, dragging Jinx off the stage.

We had a perfect spot in the front row to watch Zeke and Jericho. They really did care about each other and were happy for each other. They held hands as Sebastian read the results.

"It was a close one, but the winner of Singers is …"

I was biting my nails again. I hated when they drew this shit out, but it was for the ratings.

"Jericho Cobretti!"

I clapped and whistled as Jericho hugged Zeke firmly. I could see them both talking, Zeke congratulating Jericho. Confetti fell from the ceiling and balloons covered the crowd. Jinx wrapped me up in his arms and I held him tightly. I had everything I could possibly want, a man I loved and a career that made me happy. Life was fucking awesome. Jinx waved to someone over my shoulder and I turned to see my parents and another couple. Jinx held my hand as he welcomed them over.

Mom, Dad, *this* is Jayden." Jinx pushed me forward.

"It's so nice to meet you." I held my hand out.

"Son, we are French, come here and get your hugs!"

I got a bone-crunching hug from Jinx's father and kisses on my cheek and the same from his mother. My own parents were behind them, smiling.

"Why don't you guys all get together?" Jinx motioned to my parents. "I gotta go, babe." Jinx kissed my forehead. "Playing with the winner."

"You're leaving me with all the parentals?" I whispered to him, desperately longing to be going with him.

"You'll be fine." Jinx gave me a goofy grin.

"Okay, I'll be right here waiting."

I sat between the two sets of parents as Jinx and the Skull Blasters played with Jericho. I'd never been so proud in my life. My man could rock a drum set. Jericho and Ransom sounded awesome together, both of them with that rock 'n' roll rasp in their voices. There was yet another standing ovation as the band wrapped up, bowing before the frenzied crowd. My two weeks in California were up, but I couldn't wait to start my new life with Jinx by my side. We waited for Jinx to come back out and then he suggested we all go out to dinner to get to know one another. He leaned into my ear as we were getting into the limo.

"When we come back, I have a surprise for you."

"Another one?" I asked with a laugh. "Jinx, you've done so much already."

"Yeah? You're worth it." He slapped my ass.

Dinner was nice. My parents got to know Jinx's parents. I didn't realize Jinx was *that* French. His grandfather had been born in France, as had his father. His mother, Monique, was also French. She and Jinx's father met while they were both touring the Louvre in Paris. Jinx's father smiled a lot and spoke with his hands. My parents, on the other hand, were not very elegant, but they were on their best behavior. They didn't really have a Southern twang to their voices and I never did adopt much of one either. Since I went to school with a lot of transplants from the military, I never did get the drawl down. We drank a lot of wine and we ate a lot of bread and cheese and by ten, I was bone tired.

We separated at the hotel. Jinx's parents were staying at the same one as were my parents, courtesy of Jinx. By the time I got upstairs to the room, I was leaning on Jinx. Between the wine and fatigue, I couldn't move another step.

"Let me get it." Jinx took my key card from me.

He opened the door and turned to face me, a devilish smile playing at his lips. I frowned and stared at him.

"What did you do?"

"Come on." Jinx looked as though he were about to burst as he opened the door for me. I stopped in the middle of the room. There was a penguin on every wooden surface. The lamps were on, throwing prisms of color into every corner.

"Jinx?" My hand covered my mouth as I gasped.

"It took a long time, well, about twelve hours, but I found them all thanks to Axel and the guys. Seems they know some law enforcement dudes in Alabama and got me the names of the buyers."

I walked over to the tiny penguin on the nightstand and picked it up. It was the one with a little Santa hat and a bag of presents. I turned to Jinx with tears in my eyes.

"Oh my God. You ... you found them all? How much did this cost you?"

"It was worth every penny to see the look on your face right now. I know how precious these are to you, just like my grandfather's rock collection is to me. Some say material things are just that, but they're not. Some hold precious memories."

"Jinx." I shook my head. I had no idea how to convey how much this all meant to me.

Jinx dropped to his knees in front of me and took my hand. He stared up at me with a smile.

"I don't do romance. Well, I don't really know how. But I figured I should do what I think that person will like. I want *all* of you, Jayden. I never wanted Arielle or any of those other women the way I want you."

"Arielle," I snorted.

"I know, the only way I can remember her name is to think of a singing lobster, tritons, and fish."

"Lobster? No, Sebastian was a crab." I smiled at Jinx's face. I'd heard about his … crustacean problem from Gareth. "Too soon?"

"Ha, ha. You're ruining a good moment."

I placed the penguin back on the table and sunk to my knees in front of Jinx. I held his face in my hands and looked into his eyes.

"What you did for me, the penguins, my parents I'll never forget it, Jinx."

"Does that mean you'll take me, warts and all?" Jinx asked hesitantly.

"You have warts, too?" I asked in mock horror. Jinx sighed and I cupped his cheek. "I'm kidding. I'm nervous and I'm sorry. Yes, I'll take all of you, Josiah Jett."

Jinx made a face, but before he could protest, I kissed him. We fell back on the floor, Jinx on top of me and I arched into him, wrapping my legs around his hips.

"Want you," I moaned against his lips. "Want to do so many things to you."

"I want you to do them." Jinx wrapped his arms around my back and lifted me off the floor. We dropped onto the bed, still connected, and I kissed him hungrily. God, I *ached* for this man.

"When we get back, no more barriers. I want us to be completely together," Jinx murmured in my ear.

"Okay. So, dating? Exclusive?"

"All of the above. You're mine, Jayden."

"Show me then."

It was like I'd flipped a switch in Jinx. The animal in him came barreling out and pounced on me. Fingers sunk into me and then I was crying out, begging for more. I vaguely remembered lube and a condom, and then Jinx threw me on my back. He hovered there, panting and licking his lips as he eyed my body.

"Fuck! I want to fucking eat you!"

"Oh, I *plan* to eat you!" I growled back.

"Both times I fucked you, I couldn't see your face, wanna see it now. Want you to know who's fucking you!"

"Then fuck me, Josiah."

Fire burned through me and I cried out, hanging onto Jinx's biceps as he slammed into me over and over and over. I fucking loved every second of it. We kissed liked wild animals and Jinx pounded into my prostate as if he were earning points each time he hit that spot that would make me plummet over the edge. Two seconds later, I swear the whole hotel must have heard me because Jinx nailed it relentlessly and repetitively. I couldn't breathe or focus on anything but Jinx slamming his body into mine.

It was wild.

It was *fucking fantastic*.

I'm pretty sure my spine snapped and then I was flailing on the bed, arms and legs going this way and that as Jinx fucked me through my orgasm. I knew the very second he came; his eyes locked on mine and he bit his bottom lip. A rumble started in his chest and then a shout left his lips, his hips still bucking as he unloaded heat into my ass. He fell over on top of me and buried his face in the crook of my neck. I trailed my fingers up and down his back softly.

"Wow." I said breathlessly.

"Yeah?" Jinx lifted his head and eyed me with a grin.

"Yes. Wow."

Jinx pulled out of me carefully and went to the bathroom, emerging with toilet paper and a washcloth. I smiled at him and he looked at me with raised brows.

"What?"

"You know this never happens, right? Most guys don't do the after-care clean up. We just do it ourselves."

"You want me to stop?"

"Absolutely not. I love that you take care of me."

Jinx sat on the edge of the bed and moved a stray strand of sweaty hair from my temple.

"I want you to come home to Flagstaff with me."

"Okay. I can ask Sebastian what our schedule looks like. You know we're going on tour, right?"

"Yes, I got that much from Evander."

I sat up and leaned in to kiss him. "I want to spend as much time with you as I can."

"That night at Dick's, you said you lived around there."

"I live in Avondale."

"I'd like to see your house."

"And you will," I assured him. "But I want to see your place in Flagstaff. I like your house in Anthem."

"It'll be snowing soon in Flag."

"Snow?" My eyes widened. "I love snow! We never get snow in the South!"

"Um, if I recall correctly, you did get snow recently and Atlanta shut down."

"That was a once in a lifetime thing. Where I grew up, we never get snow. Or hardly ever."

"Ah ha! I heard some country." Jinx's brows furrowed and then his mouth dropped open. "It was you!"

"What was me?"

"The interview I heard in my car! The guy was talking about how I was his role model and ˮ

"That *was* me!" I laughed.

"Really?" Jinx caressed my face.

"Yes, I always looked up to you and when I saw you play…" I stared at him dreamily.

"The look on your face right now is incredible. I've never had someone look at me like that."

"All goo-goo eyed?"

"You're so damn cute."

"Blecch." I stuck my tongue out.

Jinx straddled me and ran his hands across my abs. "Look at this definition. You must work out."

"Not as much as you, obviously." I bit my lip and met his eyes. "Can I ask you something?"

"Sure."

"The tattoo on your back, does it … represent something?"

Jinx turned around to show me his back.

"I had it done the day after my grandfather died. It represents his flight from Earth to heaven." He spoke over his shoulder.

"It's so beautiful, Jinx," I whispered, touching the wings.

Jinx moved back over me and leaned down, brushing his lips against mine.

"I have to go somewhere tomorrow, will you go with me?"

"Of course." I nodded.

"Hey, let's take a shower."

Like I was going to turn that down.

We ended up making out more than cleaning up, but hey, I was good with that. Jinx's body wash-covered hands slid up and over my ass cheeks slowly, rubbing in circles and gripping now and then. He had fabulous hands, I loved their texture. Jinx licked my neck and lightly bit my bottom lip.

"I want to spend more time with you, time that doesn't involve a janitorial closet with unromantic bleach."

I chuckled. "I have to admit that for a few days, I got hard every time the hotel housekeeper came by with the cleaning cart." I sobered. "I'm going to spend every waking moment with you, Jinx Jett."

"Good, because I plan on doing a lot of stuff with you."

I cocked a brow with a salacious grin.

"Not that kind of stuff. Well, that kind of stuff, too," he corrected.

"I can't wait."

Chapter 17

Jinx

I was nervous as hell. Gareth stood on one side of me and Jayden on the other. He gripped my hand as we entered the garden area of the mental hospital. Rebel, Harley and Ransom had already been out to see Paul. Now it was just Gareth and me. Axel had argued that he didn't want Gareth going in without him, so Gareth had finally conceded that Axel could stay in a corner out of the way. I let Gareth go first. Paul was sitting on a wooden bench, his face lifted to the sun. We were surrounded by rose bushes in different colors, picnic tables and quiet waterfalls. Jayden and I sat down at one of the picnic tables behind Paul and watched as Gareth sat beside him.

"Is he ... okay?" Jayden asked.

"Paul? Yeah, I mean they diagnosed him with clinical depression and posttraumatic stress disorder from the car crash. He's got a long road to recovery. I think what he wants most is forgiveness."

"Forgiveness?" Jayden turned to me with a quizzical look.

I forgot we hadn't told the public who was actually behind the stalking and trying to harm Gareth after he came out. I trusted Jayden to keep the information to himself.

"This has to be kept between us." I leaned into him.

"I understand."

"Paul was the one who sent the notes to Gareth when he came out. He was the one behind everything. He wanted to be back in the band playing lead guitar and he was doing everything in his power to get there, including using our money to have experimental surgery on the hand he hurt in the wreck that ended his career."

"But Gareth had already taken over that job, and the band took off." Jayden said slowly.

"Yes, Paul was envious of Gareth, from his skills at playing guitar to Ransom's love for him. Ransom had always been overprotective of his little brother, Gareth, and Paul felt shut out when Ransom started spending more time and focus on him. The depression and P.T.S.D didn't help either. Paul did some things he would have never done otherwise."

"So you guys put him here, to protect him?"

"Yes. We knew if it got out, the media would never leave him alone and that's the last thing he needs."

I smiled as Gareth leaned into Paul, hugging him. I could tell Paul was crying.

"Gareth is a special man," Jayden said, softly.

"Yeah, he really is."

Gareth stood up and headed in our direction. He wiped his eyes and smiled at us. "He's doing well today. You should go over there now."

"You okay?" I took Gareth's hands.

"Yes. I know he's got a long road, but he's trying. Axel told me that P.T.S.D., left untreated, can become much more dangerous to the individual and those around them."

"Well, we'll go see him. We'll meet you out by the car?"

"Sure." Gareth grinned, taking Jayden's hand. "Are you coming back to Arizona with us?"

"Yes, I'm going to Flagstaff with Jinx."

"Cool, let's hang out!"

"I heard you have a treehouse." Jayden chattered excitedly.

"Dude, we have *got* to get together." Gareth slapped Jayden's back.

"You're on!"

"Okay, can we go now?" I arched a brow at Gareth.

"Go!" Gareth pushed us.

I took Jayden's hand as we crossed the grass to Paul's bench. His face was a bit pale, but all in all, he looked happy. I sat down next to him and Jayden stood off to the side. Paul's eyes lifted to mine and a genuine smile crossed his features.

"Jinx. It's good to see you. Thanks for coming to see me."

"Of course." I took his good hand.

"And who's this?" Paul motioned to Jayden.

"Paul, this is my boyfriend, Jayden Dempsey."

"Boyfriend, huh?" Paul chuckled. "I knew you swung both ways, Jett." Paul extended his hand to Jayden, who shook it carefully. "You must be something special to snag Jinx here."

"He is, Paul. He really is."

"That's good. I'm glad you found somebody, Jinx." Paul's brows furrowed. "I'm worried about Harley. I told Stan to keep one of the guys on him all the time. He's becoming more reckless, Jinx."

"I know, Paul. We're keeping someone on him 24/7, okay? Don't worry about it."

"He needs someone," Paul continued. "Someone to let him know he's there, that's he's not invisible. That he matters."

"I know," I reassured him calmly. "I'll make sure Harley's okay."

"I used to worry about you, too, Jinx, but you found someone who makes you a whole note, huh?"

I was surprised that Paul used a musical reference, although I shouldn't have been. Paul was one hell of a guitarist before the accident.

"Yeah." I looked up at Jayden. "I did."

"Ransom wants to move me to Arizona when I'm a little more stable. I think I might like that. It's kinda smoggy here."

"Well, *it is* L.A.," I chuckled.

"I just want to get better." Paul glanced at me. "I want to be me again."

"You will be. We all want that for you." I hugged him. "I miss you, man."

"I miss you, too." Paul hugged me back hard. "You guys are my family."

"And we always will be." I assured him.

We left Paul with his therapist and Jayden and I walked back to the parking lot. I broke down because I was trying to hold it together for Paul. Just seeing him like that, so wistful. Gareth put his arms around me and we both cried. Sometimes I found it hard to believe how forgiving Gareth was. Paul could have killed him with some of the accidents he arranged, but Gareth doesn't have a mean bone in his body. We pulled apart, wiping our eyes and noses.

"He bring up Harley?" Gareth snuffled.

"Yeah, and it's a legitimate concern. His parents didn't come to the show."

"No surprise there." Gareth pursed his lips and balled his fists. "Ugh! What is *wrong* with them? Don't they know " Gareth stopped and inhaled deeply, blowing out a slow breath. "I am *not* going to get upset. We'll take care of Harley."

"No, Achilles will." Axel spoke up. "And you'll let him. Achilles is a lot smarter than you know."

"Yes, well, he seems to be able to keep up with Harley and his disappearing acts," I pointed out.

"Are you guys ready to go?" Axel asked.

I took Jayden's hand and kissed him. "Yeah. I think so."

~*~

We opted to take the tour bus back home. Jayden had said goodbye to his guys, telling them that he'd see them in Arizona. I was spread out on the plush couch with Jayden between my legs as we watched the finale again. Sebastian had given us a taping and warned me not to break his guy. Turns out, Jericho asked Zeke to start a band with him and Sebastian signed on as their producer and manager. I turned my head slightly to see Harley fast asleep in the recliner, Achilles seated nearby, watching him.

"Will you tell me about Harley? Why does he need to be watched?" Jayden whispered in my ear.

"Long story but yes, I'll tell you when we get home."

Ransom chuckled across from us, watching the show. "One of these days, Rebel, that long hair is going to get wrapped around a string and get yanked out."

"Jealous of my luscious locks?" Rebel whipped his hair back and forth.

"Nah, I'm good with mine."

"Ransom, you never did tell us about your conversation with Sal Falco." I winked knowingly.

"He's a fan." Ransom shrugged.

"He seemed a little gay." I arched my brows.

"*Now* you have gaydar?" Ransom laughed. "Trust me, he's not. He's the leading man in every action flick. He's had more lip time with women than me."

"Doesn't mean jack," Rebel chimed in. "He could be using that as a front."

"What about his girlfriend?" Ransom asked. "She's always with him."

"A beard?" Jayden suggested. "You know, a woman gay men use to make people think he's straight?" Jayden clarified.

"It does happen all the time." Gareth nodded.

"No." Ransom shook his head. We all stared at him, eyebrows raised. "No! I mean, it's just not possible, okay?"

"What if he was, huh, big bro?" Gareth waggled his brows. "Would you ride the bologna pony?"

"Shut up, Gareth." Ransom threw a pillow at his brother.

"Oh yeah, Ransom would ride that beast to the altar of sin," Rebel cracked up.

"Stop *dickrespecting* Ransom," I snickered.

"This is *dickriculous*," Gareth sighed.

"Will you guys quit!" Ransom leaned over, holding his stomach in laughter. "I was with a chick that night anyway."

"Oh reallllllly?" I narrowed my eyes at Ransom. "Which one?"

"Was it the one Paul would have called Butterface?" Rebel tilted his head and thought.

"Butterface?" Jayden looked to me for explanation.

"A woman who is sexy all over. But.Her.Face. Get it? Butterface?"

"That's so mean!" Jayden slapped my bicep.

"Yeah, well, big daddy long dick over there is never hurting for women." I winked at Ransom.

"Neither were you, Superman," Ransom shot back. "But now you're domesticated and shit."

"Fuck yeah I am, and proud of it."

"We've all pounded the punanni pavement, now it's time to grow up." Rebel said, trying to keep a straight face.

Harley stretched out his arms and grinned. "Get some stankie on the hang down."

"He lives!" I laughed, throwing Harley a grin.

"How many more hours of this do we have?" Jayden asked Axel.

"A lot."

I noticed Gareth had a devilish smile in his face. I cocked a brow and narrowed my gaze at him.

"Why do you look like the cat that ate the canary?"

"Oh, nothing. I kinda knew you two would work all this shit out."

"Oh? How?"

"Dinner with Jayden. He might have said he wanted you."

"Is that right?" I leaned forward.

"Yeah, but I wanted to see you sing the Backstreet Boys." Gareth smirked.

"Ass."

"Yep."

We got to my place in Flagstaff at ten at night. Jayden and I waved to the guys as the bus rolled back down my driveway. I was dead tired even though I'd slept for a few hours. Jayden hauled his bag over his shoulder and took my hand. I was finally home and I couldn't wait to fall asleep with Jayden in my arms. I unlocked the front door and turned on the hall light. My place smelled of disinfectant, so at least I knew it was clean.

My parents and Jayden's had flown home and we promised to all get together soon. I wanted to spend as much time as I possibly could with Jayden. I went to the kitchen and grabbed two bottles of water out of the fridge. Jayden was standing in the middle of my kitchen looking around.

"Tired?" I sympathized.

"A little. I'd like to see your drum set, though."

"That I can do." I grinned, handing him his water and taking his free hand. I led him to the room where I keep my grandfather's drums. He squatted in front of them, running his fingers along the rims.

"Wow, these are in great shape. How old are they?"

"Over thirty years. My grandpa took good care of them."

"So do you." Jayden straightened and turned to face me. "You think we'll actually work?"

"I know we will. I didn't sing a boy band song to the world just to have you leave me."

"That was really brave on your part," Jayden snickered.

"I wanted you to know you're not just another notch or checkmark. You're *it*, Jayden."

"To think this all began at the mall." Jayden wrapped his arms around me.

"Then the glory hole," I laughed.

"I couldn't figure out why the guy in the next stall wasn't sticking his dick in."

"What were you doing there, anyway?"

"Relieving stress? I hadn't had sex in about eight months or so."

I whistled low and Jayden flushed.

"I'm picky, okay?" he defended.

"Um, random cock in a hole is not picky," I pointed out.

"Well, it turned out to be your fantastic cock," Jayden said huskily across my lips.

"You keep that up and I'll have to throw you down right here and make savage love to you."

"Oooh, threaten me with a good time whenever you want!"

I picked Jayden up and he wrapped his legs around my hips.

"Where are we going?" Jayden licked up my neck.

"I want to do dirty things to you," I replied, biting his bottom lip.

"Let's get in the shower, we can get dirty *and* clean."

I liked that idea. In fact, I liked it a lot. There were still a few things I wanted to do to Jayden and there were a shit ton of things I wanted him to do to me. I got him upstairs and into my bathroom, turning the water on and testing the temperature. Jayden undressed quickly, throwing his clothes in a heap on the floor. My mouth watered as I looked over his naked flesh. Jayden moved closer to me and his hands expertly flicked the button on my jeans. I lifted my arms and he removed my shirt, kissing my chest and licking my nipples, as he got busy removing my pants. My dick stood at attention, leaning as it always did and Jayden gripped me and began to stroke. We moved into the shower, Jayden still jacking me off as he tongue fucked my mouth. Fuck, the guy could kiss! I felt him everywhere, and my mind wandered back to when he fucked me, how it felt to have him inside me.

We took the showerhead down and Jayden washed me from head to toe, taking great care along my ass crack. We touched, nipped, and sucked on each other until we were ready to blow. Jayden shut off the water and we toweled off quickly, then headed for my bedroom. I barely got to the bed before Jayden shoved me down on my stomach and pulled my ass cheeks apart. I had seconds to process everything before Jayden launched an attack on my asshole.

"Oh FUCK!" I gripped the comforter and bit down on it as Jayden's tongue slid inside me. My ass arched up higher and Jayden reached beneath me to jack me off. My hips bucked into his hand as I pushed back on his tongue, which was wiggling cheerfully along my anal walls and darting in and out.

"You like that, Josiah?" Jayden licked along my perineum before diving into me again.

"God…yes! Need you!" I barely got out.

My dick was about to explode and Jayden straddled me. Somewhere in the distance of my sex-induced haze, I heard the sound of a condom package rip and then Jayden thrust his dick into my ass. I let out a cry of satisfaction and then Jayden began riding me in earnest. I was right on the edge when he was fucking my asshole with his tongue; now the fireworks were building in my balls as Jayden angled his thrusts, nailing me over and over again until I saw stars. My dick erupted on the comforter below me without help and then Jayden cried out, his body shuddering behind me as he filled me with warmth, his hips still thrusting as he rode me through his orgasm.

We laid there for what seemed like hours, breathing hard and holding each other. Jayden's lips brushed against mine seductively and I opened one eye to see him smiling at me.

"You're an animal in bed," I murmured.

"I think you like having me pound you." Jayden smiled, kissing my cheek.

"It's definitely different. I love the way it feels, though. The pressure, the burn, that full feeling and then when you hit me just right?" I shivered. "Feels so fucking good."

"I think you might just be a bottom, Jinx."

"What if I like fucking you?"

"We can do both. I'm not opposed to being a bottom. I actually like the feeling as well."

I chuckled and Jayden cocked a brow.

"What?" he asked.

"When Gareth told me he and Axel were versatile, I couldn't believe it."

"I don't see why. You love the feeling of dick in your ass."

"I like that stuffed feeling," I admitted.

"Well, I'm no anaconda, but I'm pretty proud of my guy."

"I like him. A lot." I waggled my brows.

I planned to suck Jayden's cock, just as soon as I could move again. I chuckled at the thought and Jayden smiled.

"What?" he asked.

"I have a few plans for you, sexy."

"Is that right?" Jayden nipped my lip.

"Yes, but I think we need to sleep for about twelve hours. I want to take you into town tomorrow, show you the sights."

"I'm all for that." Jayden yawned and snuggled into my chest.

I held him close, just breathing in his scent. I wanted to tell him how I felt, but not during or after sex. It needed to be said outside of the bedroom. Jayden's even breathing signaled that he'd fallen asleep. I kissed his forehead and closed my eyes.

Chapter 18

Jayden

I woke up confused for a split second, and then I remembered I was with Jinx at his house in Flagstaff. His warm body enveloped me in a cocoon of fragrances from sex to soap. He smelled edible. I snuggled into him more and kissed his neck. A low moan met my ears and then I lifted my head, kissing his chin. I kissed along his jawline while my hand kneaded his butt cheek.

"You're asking for it," Jinx mumbled, half asleep.

"Am I gonna get it?" I laughed lightly.

Jinx rolled me to my back, hovering above me with a wicked grin. His thigh moved between my legs and his fingers skated across my abs. My whole body shivered at his light touch and I inhaled sharply when Jinx wrapped his hand around my already weeping cock. His eyes held mischief and a promise of something more. He moved slowly down my torso, stopping to lick my nipple. I thrust my fingers into his hair, my hips arching up into him. Jinx chuckled across my skin, the vibrations skipping down to my nuts. I stared down at him as he licked his way down my stomach.

"Jinx?" I asked breathless.

"Mmm?"

"What are you doing?"

"Getting a taste of you."

That was all the warning I got before Jinx inhaled my prick. My eyes went wide and I yanked on his hair in complete shock. Jinx just groaned, licking around my rim and sliding his tongue around my dick. I didn't even know he could do that. He had a Gene Simmons tongue and it wrapped around the girth of my dick like a snake. Hot, molten heat slid up and down my dick as cool air hit my slit. I bit my lip to keep from screaming as Jinx rolled his tongue around my dick and then swallowed me down his throat.

"Ah fuck! Jinx … I can't ... oh fuck!"

My body jerked and then I was coming. Jinx kept at me, sucking down my seed as fast as I was shooting it. I couldn't stop staring at him. He was so fucking *hot* when he did that. Jinx pulled off, licking his lips with a smile.

"Breakfast of champions." He smiled broadly.

"Oh my God." I draped my arm over my eyes. "I can't believe you just did that."

"Well, you're negative, right?"

"Of course I am, but still. That was your first?" I asked incredulously.

"Yeah, but I did watch gay porn." Jinx's brows furrowed and then she shook his head with a laugh.

"What?" I asked.

"I probably have a lot of late fees. They're still at my house in Anthem."

I sat up with a grin. "We should watch some."

"Well, I'm not driving all the way over there for porn."

"Nah, we'll get some on my laptop. I have a subscription."

"You naughty boy!" Jinx pointed at me.

"Says the porn watcher."

"Okay, but let's get dressed so I can take you out and show you off."

"Really?" I asked uncertainly. "You want to take me out? People will see us."

"I'm pretty sure all of America saw us."

"Oh yeah." I chortled. "I think sometimes I've convinced myself that was all a dream. Kinda like the one I had of Dagger Drummond." Jinx cocked an eyebrow at me and I smiled. "Don't worry, it wasn't sexual or anything, but I have been a huge fan of those guys since the beginning."

"You really are a rocker, aren't you?" Jinx pulled me close to him.

"Yeah. Always liked that kind of music. You're so lucky you get to see those guys and talk to them!" Jinx's face broke out into a smile and I searched his eyes. "What are you thinking?"

"Nothing." Jinx grinned.

"Uh huh. I know that look." I narrowed my eyes at him.

"Come on, the day's wasting!"

~*~

We showered, dressed, and then Jinx took me into Flagstaff. We stopped at his favorite coffee place and I got a double shot of espresso. For the rest of the afternoon, I was bouncing all over the place. Jinx just laughed; he did warn me the shots were nothing to play with. He took me up to Snow Bowl and we took the chair lift across the valley and then hiked the trail. The autumn colors were vibrant all around us with yellow and orange leaves blanketing the ground. It smelled like heaven up here. I loved it.

Jinx was on the phone when I came out of the port-a-potty. He smiled at me and motioned me to come closer. As soon as I got to his side, he pulled me in and kissed my temple.

"Okay, thanks, see you soon!" Jinx hung up and kissed my nose. "You're cold."

"Nah, I'm good. It smells so good up here! Like pine and campfire."

"Some people come up here just for the view. They bring a picnic and some chairs and just stare out across the valley all day."

"It *is* beautiful. Can't wait to see it covered in snow."

"Do you ski?"

"Oh yeah, all the time in Alabama," I said wryly, elbowing him.

"We'll have to come up here together and learn."

"You don't ski?"

"Me? Ski?" Jinx laughed. "Hell no. I make snowmen and igloos. That's the extent of my snow abilities."

"Well, this should be fun. Both of us flying uncontrollably down a slippery mountainside on skinny pieces of polished   whatever they make skis out of."

"Live on the edge, I say." Jinx wrapped me up in his arms. "If you're going to spend time with me up here, we need to get you some warmer clothing."

"Can't I just snuggle and you zip me up in your jacket?"

"Mmm," Jinx kissed me and licked across my bottom lip. "That sounds good."

It wasn't hot outside, but fuck if this man didn't boil me from my balls up. We walked back to his truck holding hands. Never did I think that I'd ever meet Jinx Jett, much less that he would be my boyfriend. Jinx pushed me up against the truck and took my mouth in a heated kiss that I felt to my toes. He backed away slowly, a slight smile on his face.

"Been wanting to do that all day."

"You can do that whenever you want." I tried to come back down to Earth. Jinx's kisses were addictive. His mouth was like nothing I'd ever tasted and I wanted it all the time.

"I've got another place I want to take you."

"Lead on, baby."

"I love it when you call me that," Jinx confessed huskily against my lips.

Wow. Damn.

"Um, okay. I'll call you that all you want as long as you use that tone of voice more often."

"Oh, that won't be a problem." Jinx stared into my eyes.

I was going to fuck him on his truck if we didn't leave, like, now. I pulled away slightly and waggled my brows, jumping into the truck before he could grab me. We ended up driving back toward Flagstaff, but then Jinx took a side road and we drove for miles down a dirt road. We finally stopped in what appeared to be a camping area and Jinx jumped out, coming around to my side.

"You've got to see this view. This is where the guys and I camp."

I held Jinx's hand as we walked down a small path full of blue flowers. All around, spruce, pine, and oak trees dotted the land and big pinecones were scattered over the landscape, just begging to be made into craft projects. We came to the edge where the path became steeper downhill and Jinx stopped and pointed.

"Look," he said excitedly. "We call this the edge of the world. Well, it's also called the End of the World, but…" Jinx shrugged. "Either way? It's beautiful."

I couldn't believe what I was seeing. Down below were orange and bright red rock formations. I'd heard of them, but to see them? Breathtaking.

"See that over there?" Jinx pointed. "That's Cathedral Rock. There's Bell Rock and Courthouse Butte. If you want, I can take you down there. It's only about an hour away."

"I would love it. That is so cool."

"And the Grand Canyon maybe?"

I turned, eyes wide. "Isn't that far?"

"Nah, North Rim's only a little over an hour. We can look for rocks." Jinx waggled his eyebrows.

"I would love that," I agreed softly.

"Yeah? You wouldn't mind going rock hunting with me?"

I stepped into Jinx's arms and buried my face in his shoulder at the crook of his neck.

"I would love it."

***

Jinx kept looking over at me as we drove home. I was so tired I couldn't even keep my eyes open. I also couldn't stop yawning and I was constantly apologizing for it.

"Stop it, it's seven thousand feet up here; of course you're tired."

"Seriously?"

"Yes, so go easy on the alcohol, too. Your blood is thinned. Tomorrow night I'm taking you to the Green Room, they have the best drinks."

"Okay," I agreed, yawning again.

I didn't remember getting back to Jinx's house, or getting into his bed already naked, but I did remember Jinx pulling me close to him and kissing me lightly.

"Get some sleep, Jayden."

"Jinx, thank you for today. I had fun."

"Me too, Jayden."

Warmth wrapped around me and I was out.

~*~

Morning came and I stretched out in bed, Jinx's body draped over mine. I was so comfortable, I didn't ever want to move. Jinx's chest rose and fell and his soft breathing was like a lullaby. I leaned over and gently kissed his lips. His eyes fluttered open and then a genuine smile crossed his features.

"Hey, sexy." He stretched sleepily.

"You look good all bare-chested and naked." I licked my lips, admiring his chest.

"So do you." Jinx toyed with my bangs. "I love your boy band hair."

"Shut up," I laughed, swatting his side.

"Ow." Jinx put out his bottom lip in a mock pout.

"So," I began rolling on top of him, "the Grand Canyon today?"

"Yep." Jinx pumped his hips into me and I grinned. "We should get going. Do you have hiking shoes?"

"I have sneakers."

"That works."

***

Jinx was right. It took a little over an hour to get to the North Rim. He parked his truck and we took off along one of the trails. The weather was perfect, crisp and cool with a slight hint of a breeze. I couldn't believe the beauty before me. I kept stopping just to stare with awe at the massive canyon. There was red and pink rock dotted with green as far as the eye could see and the Colorado River flowed far below us.

"This is just...wow. I can't even come up with a word that captures all this!"

"Majestic." Jinx wrapped an arm around me. "Kind of makes you feel small, huh? Like whatever worries you have in this world pale in comparison."

"You really are a poet, aren't you?" I looked up at him.

"I haven't written anything in years."

Jinx helped me down onto a flat rock that overlooked the canyon. We both sat there, our legs hanging over the huge drop.

"I wrote a poem once for a girl, nothing special, ya know? But she laughed at it and then told all her friends."

"God, Jinx. I'm sorry."

"It was humiliating. She read it in front of everyone."

"What a bitch. Do you remember it?"

"Nah, not really. Something about comparing her face to the petals on a rose. Soft and silky or some shit like that."

"I would have loved it."

"You see that over there?" Jinx pointed across from us. "See how the clouds are really low and the sunlight penetrates them? It's like God's hands reaching into beauty. I never get tired of coming here." Jinx sighed happily.

I turned to look at him with a smile. "You feel close to your grandfather here."

"I really do. We used to come here all the time and hunt rocks. I've got crystals and minerals. I mean, I like all of them, but crystals are really pretty. My grandfather gave me an amethyst for Christmas one year and a malachite rock for my birthday. It was awesome."

I touched Jinx's cheek, he was so happy just then and full of excitement. I knew how he felt about his rocks, because that was how I felt about my penguins. We sat there for an hour, just staring out into the canyon and not speaking. We spent the rest of the walk back with our heads down, scanning for rocks. Jinx would stop, squat, pick one up and consider it carefully. It was so damned adorable, I had perma-grin.

We drove back to his house to shower and change for the bar. My muscles ached and my feet hurt, but it was the best time I'd had in a long time. Jinx wanted to take me to Sedona tomorrow, so hopefully I'd be able to move in the morning. I sat next to him in the cab of his truck and he drove with one hand, the other holding mine. He navigated the one-way roads of downtown Flagstaff and we ended up parked on the side of the road. The bar across the way was called The Green Room. Two men stood out front and another manned the door. Jinx walked up holding my hand and both men grinned. Jinx motioned to them with a smile.

"Jayden, meet Brandon and Tyler. Owners of the Green Room."

"Well, shit, if it isn't Jinx Jett. Come to crawl the floor after your regular eight Recycling Bins?" Brandon asked.

"Now you know I would never drink more than one, Brandon. Tyler likes drawing on my face with a Sharpie when I pass out."

"The penis on your forehead was a masterpiece." Tyler nodded.

I snorted and Jinx pulled me inside. A long bar occupied one side of the establishment and chairs and tables filled the rest of it. Jinx pulled me toward the back and I was surprised to see the place was much bigger. There was a stage, and the other half of the bar ended by the stage. It was a bit darker in the back, but I could see people milling around. A large group huddled right by the stage and Jinx pulled me in that direction. As we got closer, my jaw dropped as I recognized the guys from Black Ice and Ivory Tower. My hands immediately began to sweat and Jinx stopped walking, pulling me around to face him.

"What's wrong?"

"What do you mean?"

"Your hands went clammy. Are you nervous?"

"Um, hello? Black Ice and Ivory Tower are here!"

"Yeah, I know. I called them and told them I wanted them to meet my man."

"Oh. My. God," I whispered, as Dagger Drummond approached us with his guy, Ryan.

"Jinx!" Dagger wrapped an arm around Jinx's neck, tugging playfully. "Look at your guy! Isn't he just so … blond?" Dagger winked at me. "He always said he preferred brunettes."

"I did not!" Jinx balked.

"I hear you hit the skins, Jayden. Should Ashton be afraid?"

"He should be very afraid." Jinx beamed at me. "My man can rock *Moby Dick*."

"No shit?" Dagger's mouth dropped open.

I ducked my head and smiled. Jinx started dragging me and I held back.

"What are you doing?"

"I want them to hear you." Jinx started dragging me again.

"Oh my God, no! This is so embarrassing!"

"Is Jinx lying?" Dagger shot me a wicked grin.

"Hell no." I answered.

"Well, get up there and we'll back you up."

I shot a look at Jinx, who just smiled at me and encouraged me to get on stage. I couldn't believe this! I was on stage with Black Ice and Ivory Tower! Jinx dragged a stool over and sat down to the right of me. I realized the rest of the Skull Blasters had arrived and that was going to make me even more nervous. The guys counted off and I was gone in my own little world. I always blocked it all out, the screams, the chants, everything. My body moved with me, increasing the speed as my sticks moved across the skins. There was a nudge in my side and I stopped playing, looking over at Jinx.

"Um, they were done like five minutes ago." He smiled proudly.

I blinked and looked into the crowd. Everyone was clapping and raising their drinks. I stood and bowed, looking over at Jinx with a sheepish grin.

"How long was I in the zone?"

"About fifteen minutes, but fuck, you are sexy when you play! Let's get a Recycling Bin!"

Jinx led me to the bar and ordered whatever the hell he'd just said. The barkeep brought us two small pitchers with bluish/green liquid in it with a Red Bull can shoved in the ice and two straws. I cocked a brow at Jinx who eagerly began drinking the concoction. I took a sip and flavors exploded on my taste buds. It was sweet, but I could taste alcohol for sure.

"What's in it?" I asked.

"All kinds of shit, but you don't feel it until you're on your third or fourth one and then, SPLAT."

I chuckled. "Selfie! Come here!"

I snapped a picture of me and Jinx drinking out of the same pitcher. We drank more and I played with Ashton, Jinx, and Cooper Rand of Ivory Tower. I swear it felt like Christmas. We all sat around the drums and just fucked around. I'd never forget this day as long as I lived. Well, I might forget if I had one more Recycling Bin.

We closed the place down and Jinx drove us home. He'd only had one drink and ate nachos at the bar. Plus, I think I saw him sneak some water in between. Jinx was whistling some tune and I rolled my head to the side to look at him.

"Whatcha singin'?" I slurred.

"Ah, it's nothing, just some lyrics rolling around in my head. We're still banging out some tracks, so Ransom and I are putting our heads together."

"Huh…" I closed my eyes and sighed.

"Should I take you to Harley's and drop you in his pool?" Jinx chuckled.

"Is it heated?"

"Yeah. Gotta have a heated pool in Flag. It's in the shape of a guitar."

"Nuh uh!"

"Ya huh!" Jinx cracked up. "You're so cute when you're drunk."

"Eck. I hate the word cute. I guess I really do look the part of a boy bander, though."

"You are sexy as fuck, Jayden." Jinx took my hand and squeezed it.

I was almost asleep when Jinx pulled into his garage. He went around the front of the truck to my side and helped me out. I pretty much oozed out of the seat and into his arms. Jinx chuckled as he picked me up in his arms.

"I'm not a girl," I protested.

"No, you are definitely not a girl. But I don't want you to face plant on the concrete."

"You've got huge guns, Jinx," I swooned as I gripped his bicep.

I floated on a cloud of warmth through the house and then Jinx lowered me to the bed. My shoes came off and then warm hands were at the waistband of my jeans. Cool air hit my thighs before Jinx covered me with the comforter. I sighed in bliss and seconds later, Jinx was sitting me up.

"Here drink this and take these," he instructed.

"Whaisit?"

"It's water and aspirin. Preventive measure."

I drank the water and took the pills. Jinx climbed in bed and wrapped me in his arms. Then I was out.

Chapter 19

Jinx

I was sweating and the smell of alcohol permeated the sheets. I looked down at a peaceful Jayden in my arms and my nose wrinkled. He smelled like a brewery. I eyed the green glowing numbers on my clock. It was almost noon. I tried not to move Jayden too much as I got out of bed and headed for the bathroom. I leaned one hand on the wall as I pissed for what seemed like five hours. I went to the kitchen and perused my fridge and pantry for breakfast food. I found blueberry muffin mix and grinned. I went about making those and put some coffee on. Jayden rolled out of my room a half hour later, wiping the sleep from his eyes. He looked so adorable shirtless and in baggy sweats. A light dusting of blond hair decorated the valley between his pectoral muscles and trailed down his torso, wrapped around his belly button and disappeared under his sweats. I wanted to get on my knees and lick that trail.

"Jinx?" Jayden tilted his head at me, a look of confusion on his face.

I walked over to him and took him into my arms, planting a kiss on his lips and then I *did* drop to my knees. I pulled his sweats down and his eager dick popped out, bouncing against his abs. I grabbed it in my hand and bent it to my lips. Jayden's hands immediately went into my hair, tugging on it slightly as I sucked him down. Jayden's legs shook and his head was back as moans of pleasure left his lips.

"Jinx, oh God. Yeah, so fucking good!"

I swallowed him down, my throat muscles massaging his silky skin. Who knew I could deep throat?

Jayden's hips moved, pushing his dick further into my mouth and I grabbed his ass cheeks, spreading them and pulling him into my eager mouth.

"Fuck, fuck, FUUUUUCK!" Jayden howled as he shot down my throat.

I kept at him, licking around his rim and slit, sucking as much cum as I could from him. Jayden slid to the floor on shaky legs. I climbed on top of him and hovered above him, both hands planted on either side of his head.

"Good morning," I said playfully.

"Damn!" Jayden breathed. "Best wake up ever!"

"I made muffins."

"Second best wake up ever!" Jayden took my face in his hands and searched my eyes. Something was in those deep blue pools. I wanted to tell him I loved him, but part of me was still scared, was still *that* Jinx.

"Jinx…"

The timer went off on the oven and Jayden sighed. I helped him up and he followed me to the oven. I pulled out the golden brown blueberry muffins and shot a look at a drooling Jayden. I grinned and grabbed two coffee cups out of the cabinet, handing one to Jayden.

"So, Sedona today?" I asked.

"Yep." Jayden filled his coffee cup. "I want you to come to my house, too. I'm just renting it for now, but we'll see if I decide to buy it."

I wanted to tell him not to buy it, to move in with me, but my mouth wouldn't form the words. What if he said it was too soon? I know he'd be right. We'd only been together a couple of weeks. I never believed in that love at first sight shit, but I knew I loved Jayden. I loved the way his face lights up when he laughs, the way his brows furrowed when he was confused or pissed. The way he played, the way he sang, the way he walked. I loved it all.

"God, these are so good," Jayden moaned around a mouthful of muffin.

"We'll be fighting over the last one," I laughed.

"Let's take them with." Jayden grabbed a muffin and headed for my room. "I'll be ready in five."

"Okay." I called after him. Then I hid the last muffin in the microwave.

We took the Eighty-Nine to Sedona, winding through the mountains. It was a spectacular view. We actually parked off to the side of the road when we got to Slide Rock. It was October, but there were still people milling about and taking pictures of the waterslides carved out from red sandstone.

"Wow, this is beautiful," Jayden enthused.

"We need to come back in the summer. This place is packed, but for good reason. It's fun as fuck."

"I'll keep that in mind." Jayden smiled, taking my hand.

We continued on to Sedona and I slowed down on the main road in, letting Jayden take a good look at all the small shops along the way. I found a parking spot and Jayden and I hit the sidewalk holding hands.

"Wow, it's so gorgeous out here." Jayden glanced around at all the restaurants.

"Hungry? We could have some rattlesnake."

"Seriously?" Jayden's eyes widened.

"Yup. There's a place over there that serves buffalo and cactus fries."

"Fuck it," Jayden laughed. "I'm in."

We ate lunch and Jayden informed me that rattlesnake tasted like chicken. I thought everything tasted like chicken if it was something you wouldn't normally eat. We headed to Bell Rock because it was really the only formation easily accessible. Jayden and I began the hike up the side, looking for rocks along the way.

"Wow! Look at the view!" Jayden cried excitedly. "Okay, there's some pretty scenery, but there's nothing like *this* in Alabama! Let's take a selfie!"

"There's that drawl again." I laughed as Jayden swatted me. I stood with him and he snapped the red rock formations behind us.

We sat on a rock overhang and stared out across the red rocks. Jayden took my hand and kissed me. I know what he was thinking because it was what I was thinking, too. He'd be leaving soon, going on tour with London Boys. I wrapped an arm around him and we sat there until the sun set, the sky overflowing with pink, orange, and lavender.

"Will you come to my house tomorrow?"

"I'll go with you anywhere," I answered immediately.

"You were going to tell me about Harley." Jayden saw my face and backpedaled. "You don't have to."

"No, if you're going to be in my life, you need to know about my friends. Harley is complicated. His home life, well, let's just say he's almost invisible."

"What do you mean?"

"Harley was a surprise. His father had a vasectomy after their firstborn, so Harley was unexpected. His older brother, Holden, was the apple of his parents' eyes. The jock, the straight-A student, and then he joined the Army." I sighed. "Holden was killed in combat about three years ago and Harley has never recovered from it. I've been to his parents' house. They're like zombies and they never really acknowledge Harley's presence."

"Oh God." Jayden shook his head sadly.

"That's why he's always acted out. What do they say? That even negative attention is better than no attention? He's trying to be *seen*, but I don't think his parents have ever fully recovered from the loss of Holden, either. It's like they lost one son and forgot they had another one. The guys and me, we try to spend as much time with Harley as we can, but it's going to take a lot more than us. We can't be with him all the time."

"That's why Achilles is with him, right?"

"We should have done it a long time ago." I shook my head. "We just thought we were enough. I guess you always need your parents."

"I guess so." Jayden agreed. "Mine hurt me, but they're trying now."

"They love you. I saw it when I was at their house."

"Yeah, they said you grilled them."

I smiled. "Yeah, I might have."

"What you did…" Jayden trailed off, swallowing hard.

"I would do it all over again, Jayden," I said softly. "You deserve it."

Jayden and I made out on the overhang until the stars came out and lit up the sky. I didn't want to leave, but I knew the days with Jayden were dwindling down. We drove back to the house in Flag and I packed a bag for Jayden's.

He made love to me again and I fell asleep with him in my arms.

It was becoming a habit.

We stopped at the store on our way into Avondale. I bought chocolate, crackers, and marshmallows along with some muffin mix and dinner staples. Avondale was on the outskirts of Phoenix and Jayden's house was at the end of a dead end street. His backyard overlooked Garden Lakes, which was an actual lake surrounded by houses. Most of them had docks with small boats moored to them. Jayden's house was white with red clay tile on the roof. It was cute and homey. Jayden unlocked the door and I stepped down into a sunken living room with a fireplace in one corner and built-in bookshelves along another wall. I stepped up to the shelf and looked at the book titles. They ranged from Shakespeare to male romances. I cocked a brow at one of them.

"Assassin Shifters?"

"Oh God, yeah! My favorite series of all time! You've got to read them! There are some hunky assassins in those books."

"Seriously?" I turned to him with one of the books in my hands. "Assassin werewolves?"

"Just read one, ya skeptic!"

"Fine. I will read one while we eat s'mores."

Jayden was practically bouncing up and down. "I can't wait till you read it! We'll have so much to talk about."

"We don't talk now?" I arched my brows.

"You know what I mean."

"Let's start a fire." I crossed the room to the fireplace.

"It's eighty degrees outside!" Jayden balked.

"It'll cool off to the lower seventies. I hope."

"Let's grill dinner first. We can sit outside on the dock and eat."

"Sounds like a plan."

***

There was a reason I lived in Anthem. It was quieter and further away from the airport. Phoenix was nice, but it was big and getting crowded.

"Are there even fish in this lake?" I asked doubtfully.

"Yes, bass and catfish," Jayden answered, biting into his ribs.

We'd gotten a rack of ribs at the store plus salad fixings and potatoes. Jayden was a mess of BBQ sauce and I licked the side of his mouth. Jayden turned and our lips met, spreading sauce all over both of us. We pulled back from the kiss, both of us panting. I grabbed another rib from the plate and lifted it to Jayden's lips, covering them with sauce. Jayden moaned softly as I licked across his lips, nipping at his lower one.

"Hmm, maybe we should take the ribs to my bed and have fun."

"Just the sauce." I gave him my best leer.

"Bring your cuffs?"

"Nope. I didn't think about it."

"I've got rope."

"Hmm, are you into bondage?"

"Nah. I can't get into BDSM or threesomes."

"Good, because I don't share and not really into ball gags or floggers."

"We are so, um, plain," Jayden laughed.

"I know, I was kidding around with Gareth and gave him a sex swing."

"Now that I could get into." Jayden fell back laughing.

"I want to spend every waking moment with you, in bed or out, don't care. Just want to be with you as long as I can."

"Me too." Jayden leaned in and I met him halfway. We kissed slowly, relishing in the taste of each other. "I don't want to leave."

"We knew this was coming. Did you hear from Sebastian?"

"Yes, I did. I didn't know how to bring it up. I leave in two days, Jinx."

My heart sank and I pulled Jayden into my arms. I inhaled his scent, touched his soft skin.

"We'll make this work, Jayden," I promised him.

***

I walked around Jayden's house, smiling at his collection of penguins scattered about. Jayden was in the shower cleaning off all the BBQ sauce I'd managed to cover him in. We had an interesting sex life. I chuckled and fingered one of his penguins. There were two of them, one was offering up a pebble to the other.

"That's my favorite," Jayden called from behind me.

I turned to find him wearing a towel around his waist, water dripping through that fine dusting of chest hair.

"Yeah?"

"Adelie penguins are the ones that search for the pebble to give to their mate," Jayden explained as he approached me. He took the crystal penguin off the shelf and smiled, handing it to me. "I want you to have it."

"I couldn't." I shook my head.

"You can. I don't want you to forget me while I'm gone."

"That's not going to happen."

"I can promise you this, Jinx. You're it for me. I won't be with anyone but you."

"I can promise the same thing. We *will* make it, Jayden. I've never felt like this for anyone."

"Ditto," Jayden whispered as he leaned in to kiss me.

I didn't know how I was going to make it without him, but I had a job to do, too. I had a record to make. I'd just have to stay busy. Jayden was crawling up my body, his kisses becoming more forceful. He wrapped his legs around me and delved into my mouth. I carried him to the bedroom and removed his towel. Jayden spread his arms and legs out, looking wanton and hedonistic. I kissed his hip and slid down, my tongue trailing across the side of his dick. His hips arched, begging for more. I grinned and straddled him, wrapping my fingers around his dick. I stroked him slowly, my mouth fucking his as I did. Jayden whimpered, his dick flexing in my hand. I pulled him into my lap and wrapped my arms around him, kissing his shoulder and sucking on the skin at his collarbone.

"Yeah, mark me," Jayden rasped.

Somehow, we managed to get a condom and I fucked Jayden slowly, holding him in my arms as I thrust into him over and over. The noises he made and the looks he got were something I'd always remember. Jayden groaned into my neck as I hit him hard, his fingers sinking into the flesh on my back. Fuck, that turned me on!

"Jinx..." Jayden moaned.

"I know," I whispered into his ear. I angled my hips and hit him at different angles, each time sinking in further and further. Jayden came with a loud, drawn-out shout and I followed seconds later. We got cleaned up and then I tumbled into bed, reaching for Jayden. He came to my side and wrapped himself around me.

"Jinx?"

"Yeah?"

"I'm going to miss you."

"Ditto."

Chapter 20

Jinx

Two days later, I was saying goodbye to Jayden at the airport. I held him as long as I could, reassuring him that he was the only one for me. I'd never been the faithful kind; hell I'd never been more than the one night kind. Jayden changed all of that. We'd spent every night making love and taking pictures. Jayden had a thing about selfies. I guess it was a youth thing. Damn, I suddenly felt old!

Jayden pressed something cool into my hand and then he was off, walking through security. The reality of it hadn't hit until his warmth left me. I opened my hand and looked at the stone in my palm. My head snapped up and I caught Jayden smiling at me from beyond the security checkpoint. I pressed my fingers to my lips and sent him a kiss. Jayden grinned, pretending to grab it in the air.

God, I was so fucked and apparently dickless. Fuck it.

I left the airport in a daze, not quite sure where to go or what to do. I walked out to the parking lot to find Ransom, Gareth, Harley, and Rebel smiling at me. I stopped walking and looked behind me, then looked back at them.

"What's all this?"

"We thought you could use some down time with us." Gareth approached me, grabbing me in a hug.

I hugged him back and squeezed my eyes shut. Fuck, I was *not* going to cry.

"Whatcha got there?" Harley motioned to my closed fist.

"Jayden gave me a pebble," I answered robotically.

"A pebble?" Rebel tilted his head in confusion.

"Oh God! That's so sweet!" Gareth exclaimed.

"Explain?" Ransom's brows furrowed.

"Jayden is like, totally into penguins. Well, Adelie penguins offer their mate a pebble and then they are mates for life." Gareth turned to me. "He gave you *his* pebble. I saw it when I was in his hotel room. It was in this really pretty box."

I ran my fingers over the smooth stone with a smile. I knew exactly what I was going to do with it.

"Come on, let's keep you occupied, yeah?" Rebel grabbed me around the shoulders. "You look like you might cry. Don't worry, you're rich and we have a jet."

I laughed.

~*~

Halloween found me at the Green Room with the guys. They were trying to keep me busy. I'd already gone shopping with Harley for new clothes, out to lunch with Ransom and to the firing range with Rebel. The man did love his weapons. I sat playing with the straws in my Recycling Bin, wishing Jayden was here with me to drink it. Brandon, the owner, eyed me over the bar and a small smile graced his lips.

"A penguin, huh? That wouldn't be for your boybander, would it?"

I pulled my penguin bill up and shot him a look. "Yes, it is. He's Skyping me tonight, and I wanted him to see my costume."

"He's sooo FLUFFY!" Gareth squealed behind me.

I turned on the stool and had to laugh. Gareth was dressed as a Navy SEAL, Axel was at his side dressed as a rocker.

"Oh my God," I cackled. "You guys are hilarious!"

"Yeah? Well, Rebel is Cousin Itt from the Addams family."

"Aw, Axel. I thought for sure you'd come as Lurch." I winked.

"Harley is Gomez," Axel informed me.

"And Stan is Morticia." Gareth snickered.

"Are you serious?" My eyes widened.

"Yep, he looks pretty," Gareth nodded. "Ransom came as Pugsley."

"Oh shit. I gotta see this!" I jumped from the stool and checked out the back of the club. Sure enough, Stan sat next to Harley, his legs encased in fishnet stockings and six-inch stilettos on his size 11 feet. Long, black hair cascaded down his back.

"Stan?"

He turned and shot me a sultry look. His face was pale white and his lips were blood red. He broke into a smile.

"Hey, Jinx! Love the costume. Aren't you hot, though?"

"How did I miss you guys coming in?" I tilted my head, admiring Stan's long legs. "Did you shave?"

"We came in through the back door and yes, I did shave."

"Dude." I shook my head.

"I can't have black leg hair sticking out of my fishnets. Not very feminine."

"So, you two make a sexy couple," I joked as I nudged Harley.

"Well, I dragged this out of the closet. I figured why not? Last year I was Captain Jack Sparrow."

"Yes, I did love your accent. Savvy?" I grinned.

"I have that itch!" Harley announced suddenly. He shook his hands out. "Gotta play!"

"Yeah? I got a song in mind." I walked up to the stage and took the steps two at a time. I grabbed the microphone and turned it on. "Where are my guys? Let's get up here and have a God complex."

Harley laughed and bounded up the stairs, followed by Ransom, Gareth, and Rebel. We made an impressive group at that moment, dressed as we were. I had to squeeze my waddly penguin ass behind the drum set on stage. Gareth and Harley faced me and I hit my sticks together. I started to play and then Harley turned to the mic. He doesn't sing solo often, but this song was his favorite. Fall Out Boy's 'Sugar We're Going Down'. I noticed our bodyguards at the bar talking with Stan and as soon as Harley opened his mouth, Achilles spun around. I had to smile; the guy probably didn't realize Harley could sing.

I felt free again. Music always took me away; it, along with Jayden, was my drug. I pounded the skins as Harley sang, with Gareth and Ransom backing him up. Most of the bar was now in front of the stage singing with us. We loved this part, coming home and playing in our hometown. No matter how famous we'd become, we were still the guys they knew before we hit it big. And we might play hard-core metal, but we also liked other kinds of music. The bar went nuts as we finished, everyone clapping and whistling. The five of us bowed and I grabbed the microphone.

"Drinks on me!"

That got another raucous round of applause and screams. I looked at the time and excused myself. I had about two minutes before Jayden called. I couldn't wait to hear his voice. I missed him so much. I stood outside the bar, pacing the sidewalk. Thank God I was wearing my penguin costume because it was fucking freezing. My phone jingled and I smiled. Jayden's face lit up my screen and I almost sighed.

"Oh my God!" Jayden laughed. "I love it! You look so cool!"

"Yeah? I got one for you for next year. We can go together." I peered at the screen. "You look so tired."

"I am," Jayden sighed. "I didn't know it would be this hard. I'm exhausted, Jinx."

"You need to eat right and drink lots of juice, okay? Your body isn't used to the time changes and different climates, so take care of your immune system."

"I had a blueberry muffin this morning." Jayden winked.

"So did I. It wasn't the same without you."

Jayden looked around and lowered his voice. "I don't know if I can do this, Jinx. I wasn't prepared for the concerts, the fans, the lack of sleep."

"You can, Jayden. Those people waited in line and some refreshed their screen over and over to get tickets to see you. They made you who you are. I know it's hard, but you owe them to be at your best."

"I know." Jayden grinned. "Thanks, I needed to hear that. Any chance I'll see you soon?"

"I have a few more tracks I need to bang out, but it's moving along pretty fast. I really need to see you, too."

"I haven't been with anyone, I promise you that," Jayden assured me.

"Neither have I, and I won't be."

The door to the bar opened and Gareth sauntered out, taking a deep breath of fresh air. He spotted me and walked over. He leaned into the screen and a smile rose to his lips.

"Hey, Jayden! How are you?"

"Is that Axel?" Jayden joked.

"Ha ha." Gareth pointed at the screen. "You looked wiped."

"I really am," Jayden admitted.

"Look, I can give you some pointers since I'm the sickly one of this group."

"Thanks, Gareth. I appreciate it. Can you email me? I have to get some sleep now if I'm going to make it through tomorrow."

"You bet." Gareth winked and went back inside the bar.

"Hey," I said softly. "Get some rest okay? Happy Halloween, Jayden."

"Happy Halloween, my penguin."

~*~

Thanksgiving arrived and I was with my parents. Harley was in the kitchen with my mother, making rolls from scratch. God forbid we actually bought already-made rolls. My mother would have a fit. I mixed the stuffing ingredients as I kept an eye on Harley. He was laughing at something my mother said. It was good to hear him laugh.

His own parents were just sitting around today when I went to get him. They barely acknowledged him as he left. My mother swiped some flour from Harley's cheek and kissed his forehead. My heart ached for him. I was lucky that my parents loved me, acknowledged me, accepted me. I looked over my shoulder to see Achilles sitting in a recliner next to my father, both watching a football game in total concentration.

Achilles had called me in the morning to see if I was going to invite Harley over and, of course, I had to tell him that I have invited Harley every year for Thanksgiving. I wasn't sure Achilles knew everything about Harley. But I was getting the distinct impression that he knew quite a bit since he wouldn't leave Harley by himself.

My phone chimed in my pocket and I rushed to wipe my hands clean. I stepped out back as I answered Jayden's call. He looked better; his face had color and his eyes were bright.

"Hey sexy." I smiled at him.

"Hi. Happy Thanksgiving!"

"Back atcha. Have you heard from your parents?"

"Sure did. Called me at one in the morning," Jayden laughed.

"I'm glad they called. Did you have some turkey?"

"I had turkey and all the fixin's! Sebastian made sure I got my American Thanksgiving."

"What about the twins?"

"Nah, they're Greek. They had gyros."

"Aw, that's just wrong," I winked.

My mother leaned over my shoulder and waved at my phone.

"Happy Thanksgiving, Jayden!" she all but yelled.

"Thank you, Mrs. Jett!"

"Please Jayden, call me Monique, or maybe, Mom?" my mother winked.

"Ma!" I balked. "Stop pushing!"

Jayden cracked up and I shot him a glare. "Stop that."

"Why? My mother pretty much said the same to you."

She had. When I'd called them recently, Jayden's mother had dropped hints left and right about marriage. I was never sure if I was the marrying type, but for Jayden? I'd do it. I scrunched my brows in thought and Jayden cleared his throat. I looked at my phone to see him smiling.

"What?" I asked.

"Are you thinking Jayden Jett or Jinx Dempsey?"

"I wasn't —"

"Oh yeah, you were," Jayden flirted. "Don't worry, I'll change mine to Jayden Dempsey-Jett."

"You'd do that?" I asked incredulously.

"HA! You *were* thinking about it!"

I laughed and Jayden winked at me. I missed him so damn much it hurt. Jayden seemed to read my mind because in the next instant he touched his phone screen.

"I miss you, too."

"I'm going to see you soon, I promise," I assured him.

"I …need you, Jinx." Jayden blushed.

"Me too. Soon."

"I gotta go to bed. We'll be in Tokyo soon and the time changes are still fucking with me."

"Get some rest."

"Hey, Jinx?"

"Yeah?"

"Eat a drumstick for me."

"I will if I can get to it. Harley and my dad usually grab them before I do."

"Trip them," Jayden suggested.

"You are so evil. I love it."

"Night, babe."

My heart flipped at the endearment and I smiled. "Night."

~*~

Jayden had been gone for two months and I was losing my mind. We talked every night via Skype and we texted all the time, but it wasn't the same. I had his pebble made into a leather corded choker necklace. I wore it all the time. I sighed in frustration as I waited for the guy at the rock shop to finish making my surprise for Jayden. My phone beeped and alerted me to a new email. I stood outside and opened it. It was a video from Jayden. Ed Sheeran's 'Photograph' began to play and pictures of me and Jayden danced across the screen. There was video of Jayden with his guys holding up my picture, a picture of Jayden asleep on a plane with my picture against his chest. Pictures mixed with video splashed across my phone screen and I realized I'd started crying. Fuck, I was so gone for this guy it was ridiculous.

My heart ached as I listened to the lyrics of the song. I wasn't going to wait for him to come home. I was going to go to him, like, now. I finally got my present for Jayden back from the rock guy and headed back to my house. I packed enough clothes for a month and then I went to

Ransom's. Harley and the guys were sitting around the table as I entered. They took one look at me and laughed.

"I wondered how long you could hold out." Gareth chortled.

"I'm sorry if this fucks up the new record." I began my apology but didn't get far.

"Shut up. We've got this, okay?" Harley stood up and walked over to me. "Go to him, Jinx. I've never seen you so happy and miserable at the same time."

"You going to be okay?" I took Harley's hand. "I can stay."

"Nope." Harley shook his head. "I'll be fine. We all will, you go get your man!"

"I love you guys, you know that right?" I opened my arms up for them all.

"You love me the most." Harley grabbed me and held me tightly. "I'm so happy for you," he whispered in my ear.

"I'll be back soon, okay? You listen to whatever Achilles says."

"Yeah right!" Harley chuckled in my arms.

"Group hug!" Gareth plowed into me.

I hugged them all and we laughed. I took a step back and looked at them. We would bleed for each other. I'd never been so happy to have these guys.

"Get outta here." Rebel pushed me in the ass.

"Tell Jayden we said hi." Ransom added.

"I will."

~*~

I called Sebastian and arranged to meet up with them after the concert. There was a huge party at some fancy hotel in Tokyo where the guys would be taking pictures with fans and signing autographs. I took a cab from the airport and was dropped off in front of the hotel where Sebastian was waiting for me. He hugged me and I hugged him back, pulling away with a look of surprise. Sebastian just smiled and took my hand, walking with me into the hotel.

"I'm glad you came, Jinx. Jayden's been missing you."

"Yeah? Well, I missed him, too." I fingered the rock around my neck.

"He's done for the night. Here's the room key."

"Thanks, Sebastian."

I boarded the elevator and my whole body thrummed with excitement. After two months, I was going to see Jayden. I found the room and slid the key card. The door opened and I cocked an ear for any sounds. The shower was running and I grinned as I began removing my clothes before I headed for the bathroom. I cracked the door to the bathroom and gasped. Jayden was behind a clear shower door, his soapy hands running up and down his body. I threw the rest of my clothing on the floor and waited until Jayden turned his back to me. I slid open the door quietly and stood behind him, just admiring the view. My hands finally moved and I placed them on his shoulders.

"Hey!" Jayden shouted, elbowing me in the face.

"Ow! Fuck man!" I rubbed my eye.

"Jinx?!" Jayden squealed in astonishment.

"Um, yeah. Surprise?"

"Holy shit!" Jayden jumped on me and kissed me.

I held him close, groaning at the taste of the man I loved. Jayden coiled around me tightly, his hands threading into my hair as he kissed me deeply.

"Missed you so much," he breathed between kisses.

"I couldn't stay away any longer," I replied in the same fashion.

"Missed your lips, hands, everything!" Jayden plunged into my mouth and I pushed him up against the shower wall. "Want you now."

We'd already talked about our test results; we were both negative, so I wasn't opposed to taking him on the shower wall, but lube or something would be nice. I didn't want to hurt him. As if hearing my thoughts, Jayden reached an arm behind me, motioning to the shower shelf.

"Lube," he grated.

"You have lube in the shower?"

"Don't judge, just fuck."

I grabbed the bottle and Jayden spread some on his hand. He lubed up my dick and then positioned himself right above my hard cock. Our eyes met as he slid down my length.

"Ohhh fuck, missed you!" Jayden choked out.

I gripped Jayden's ass cheeks as I thrust up into him. His arms wrapped around my neck and we kissed as I filled him, thrusting harder and harder on each in-stroke. It was like we were never apart; we clicked right back into place. Jayden's legs tightened around my hips and he moved his body with mine, both of us inhaling heavily through our noses as we kissed. It didn't take me long, I was bareback and Jayden's ass clamped down on me like a vice, massaging me with molten heat. I came crying out, gripping Jayden tightly as my orgasm shot into his ass. Jayden came seconds later, his dick erupting on my abs and chest. We stayed under the spray for a while until the water turned cold. I helped Jayden dry off and we moved to the master suite. Jayden fell on the bed and held his hand out to me. His eyes widened and he sat up.

"Is that my pebble around your neck?"

"Yeah, I hope you don't mind, but I wanted it on me all the time." I crossed the room to my suitcase. "I have something for you." I removed my gift for Jayden and placed it on the bed next to him. "Go ahead, open it."

Jayden took great care untying the bow and he cracked the lid of the box open. His eyes filled with tears as he picked up the malachite penguin figurine I'd had made for him out of my grandfather's rock.

"Jinx …" Jayden ran his fingers over the fine lines engraved in stone. "It's so beautiful."

"I got something else for you," I exclaimed, grabbing the necklace out of my bag. "It's from the same malachite rock. I made it into a necklace like mine."

Jayden wiped at his eyes and looked up at me. "Can you put it on me? I'm never going to take it off."

"Aren't we a mushy pair?" I chuckled, putting the choker on him.

"If you want to be a badass, we can say they're collars."

"Nah, I'm good with it. One more thing, though." I stepped back a bit from the bed and got on my knees. I'd written the poem two months ago for Jayden and had been tweaking it ever since. I just hoped I remembered it all. I cleared my throat and Jayden sat on the edge of the bed, anxiously waiting to hear what I had to say.

"When I was scared, you soothed me. When I was lost, you found me. When I was unsure, you reassured me. This I promise you; when you are frightened, I will be there. When you are lost, I will light the way. When you are unsure, I will hold your hand. All these things I will keep true, because more than anything, I love you."

Jayden jumped on me, knocking me on my ass. He peppered my face with kisses.

"I love you, too! I thought you got that, though, when I gave you the pebble."

"I'm dense, ya know. Actions speak louder than words. I know that."

"How long are you staying?" Jayden snuggled into my neck.

"As long as the band lets me. I packed for a month, but I can stay longer if you want."

"I want."

We got in bed and just stared at each other. I never thought I could love someone as much as I loved him. He loved me, baggage and all, and I loved my little boy bander. What were the odds?

"Hey, Jayden?"

"Yep."

"What kind of car do you drive?"

"A Lamborghini Countach. Why?"

"Just wondering if you'd like to park it in my garage."

Jayden chuckled on my chest and I peered down at him.

"What?" I asked.

"Is that sexual innuendo?"

"No, I want you to move in with me. I mean, if you want to."

"Yeah, I do." Jayden touched my cheek with a smile. "I got my penguin in more ways than one."

"Yeah, yeah ya did."

And I got mine.

THE END

Sneak Peek

Chapter 1

HARLEY

The TV was blasting in the living room as I headed into the kitchen with the groceries I'd just bought for my parents. They were watching Wheel of Fortune or something like that. Neither one even acknowledged my presence as I walked right by them. Nothing new there. I could bring in the whole marching band from the school along with a herd of elephants and they wouldn't bat an eyelash. I put the stuff away and then headed upstairs. I faltered on the last step as I noticed my older brother's bedroom door was slightly ajar. That never happens, his room was a shrine. I took the last step and crossed to his door, opening it the rest of the way. Nothing was moved, everything still in its place. My mother dusted in here every week and puts everything back right where it was, just in case he came home.

He wasn't coming back home. Not ever, because Holden Payne was killed in Afghanistan.

My heart ached as I ran my fingers across his desk. The picture of the two of us astride his Harley motorcycle was still sitting there. God, I missed Holden. Not that my parents paid me any mind before he passed away. I was the surprise. Even after my father's vasectomy, I still made it through. Holden made things … tolerable. We did stuff together. He took me places and always doted on me because he knew my parents didn't even know I was alive.

Should I have hated him for being their favorite? Maybe, but I didn't. Holden was my mom *and* my dad blended into one.

Now I just felt alone.

I shut his door behind me as I left, and wandered into my old room, which was now the sewing/workout room. Amazing how I bought the house for my parents, paid their bills and the groceries, but I didn't have a room.

Oh, that was right. I didn't exist.

I'd moved out right after Holden died. Why stay? He wasn't there anymore and as much as I tried to convince my parents to move, to get away from the memories, they declined. I headed back to the living room, my parents still watching their show. Pictures of Holden were scattered all over the room, from his childhood to his Army picture. A neatly folded American flag in its oak case graced our fireplace mantel. Holden was everywhere and I had to get out.

"Okay, I'm headed back to my house," I said as loudly as I could.

I got a slight wave of my father's hand and that was it.

I hung my head and grabbed my jacket and keys off the table by the front door. It was almost Christmas and I was going to spend it with my Skull Blasters bandmates: Ransom Fox, his brother, Gareth Wolf, and Rebel Stryker. Oh, and with the bane of my existence   Achilles, the bodyguard from hell.

I was really missing Jinx Jett right now, but he was off with his boyfriend, Jayden Dempsey, on his London Boys tour. Jinx was our drummer, and a former man-whore. He'd met Jayden for the first time at a mall and given him an autograph. The second time? Well, that story was a lot more interesting. They met at a gay bar and Jinx was trying out a glory hole for the first time. He worked up the nerve to put his dick in. Jayden was the receiver of said dick. The third time they met was the clincher. Jayden was part of London Boys, a boy band, and Jinx purely hated boy bands. After spending two weeks together in California, Jinx and Jayden got closer. Now they were in love.

I was happy for my best friend, don't get me wrong, but I missed him in my life. Jinx called a lot and we Skype, but there was a void in my life now. I stepped out into the garage and stopped in front of Holden's motorcycle. He and my dad had a thing for Harleys and so, here I was, Harley James Payne. I'd tried to take the bike out and that was about the only time my father said anything to me. He screamed at me not to touch it.

Holden would hate it, his bike gathering dust three years after his death. He would want me to ride it, he'd want me to take it on the curves in Camp Verde and Black Canyon. I touched the chrome metal and smiled. We had good times on this bike, him and I. I pushed the memories aside and walked out into the driveway. There, perched on the hood of my truck, was Achilles. I cursed and he jumped off the hood, striding over to me in two steps. Damn, the man was tall.

"Harley." Achilles stood over me.

"You know, I *hate* that tone of voice." I looked up at him. "I'm not a child."

"Then stop acting like one."

"How did you find me this time?" I folded my arms across my chest and gazed up at him. Achilles was what I would call an Adonis. He belonged in a museum of art. His chiseled jawline and straight nose complement his high cheekbones. His eyes, on the other hand   well, they were hard to describe. They reminded me of blue quartzite, but there was some gray in there with a little …

"I'm former Special Forces, Harley. I can find a pin in a haystack."

"Well, that would take time, now wouldn't it?"

"Yes, but you seem to think you're Harry Potter."

I blinked. "Huh?"

"Get this through your thick skull, Harley. I'm not leaving your side."

Why did that thrill me *and* annoy me?

"Even if I had a pocketful of fucks, I still wouldn't give you one," I tossed flippantly over my shoulder as I approached my truck. A strong hand gripped my bicep and then I was a hair's breadth from Achilles' face.

"Don't ever think you can shake me, Harley Payne. You got that? And drive slower! Are you trying to kill yourself?"

"Yes, Achilles," I agreed wryly.

"It's not funny." Achilles leaned even closer to me and my hair stood up on the back of my neck. "I'm responsible for you; do you know what that means?"

"Is it that Chinese proverb thingie?"

"No." Achilles sighed, rubbing his face with his hands.

Jesus, the guy's biceps were bigger than my thighs. He could probably break a brick with his thighs, come to think of it …

"Harley!"

"Wha?!"

"Are you listening to me?"

"Yup."

I was trying, though. Achilles searched my eyes and I swear sweat dripped down my back. What was it about this guy that sets me on edge? His hand rose and hovered by my face. The wind rustled the trees and then Achilles blinked and stepped back from me.

"Go home, Harley," he instructed as he walked down the driveway.

"Should I set a place for you at the dinner table?" I called jokingly.

Achilles stopped and looked over his shoulder. "Yes. You should."

I started at that. Achilles doesn't come in my house, at least I didn't think he did. What did I know? He'd probably painted himself onto my wall like Rambo did in the movie with mud.

"French fries or tater tots?" I tried to keep it light, although I was shitting my pants.

"Neither. Baked potato. And don't worry, I'll get the groceries."

"How do you know I have potatoes?"

"In the pantry, bottom shelf."

"Ah ha!" I pointed. "You *have* been in my house."

Achilles walked back to me and leaned into my face again. "I am everywhere, Harley. Don't forget it."

I stood there and stared as Achilles walked away again. Why did that man infuriate me *so much?*

And why was I staring at his ass?

Start the ride from the beginning with: A Marked Man; Alaska with Love; By the light of the Moon; Half Moon Rising; Best Laid Plans; For the Love of Caden; The General's Lover; Russian Prey; An Ignited Passion; Reflash; The Red Zone; Irish Wishes; Pleading the Fifth ; Betrayed; Summer of Awakenings; Into the Lyons Den; The Nik of Time and The Littlest Assassin-Shifters; Lessons Learned; Broken Bonds and Forbidden; Dirty Ross; Savage Love and Locke and Key

The 12 Olympians: Justice for Skylar; At Year's End; Lux Ex Tenebris; Strange Addiction and Ryde the Lightning

From Wilde City Publishing: A Betting Man ; A Marrying Man and A Fighting Man; A Working Man and A Healing Man

The Medicine and The Mob; An Eye For an Eye and The Harder they Fall

The Rock Series: FRET

And, Second Time Around and Gabriel's Fall
Join me on my Facebook pages!
https://www.facebook.com/authorsandrine.g.dion
https://www.facebook.com/pages/Official-Sandrine-Gasq-Dion/137320826386776?ref=hl
@Sandrine_GasqD

https://sites.google.com/site/assassinshiftertree/

Made in the USA
Charleston, SC
18 May 2016